# Elsie's Life Lessons:

## Walking in the Fruit of the Spirit

A Study Guide Based on
Books One and Two of the
*A Life of Faith: Elsie Dinsmore* Series

Written by
Elizabeth DeBeasi

MCP
Mission City Press
Franklin, Tennessee

| | |
|---|---|
| Cover & Interior Design: | Richmond & Williams, Nashville, Tennessee |
| Cover Photography: | Michelle Grisco Photography, West Covina, California |
| Typesetting: | BookSetters, White House, Tennessee |

For more information, write to Mission City Press at P.O. Box 681913, Franklin, Tennessee 37068-1913, or visit our web site at:

# www.alifeoffaith.com

Library of Congress Catalog Card Number: 00-107360
Mission City Press
Elsie's Life Lessons: Walking in the Fruit of the Spirit
ISBN #: 1-928749-51-8

Printed in the United States of America
2 3 4 5 6 7 8 — 06 05 04 03 02 01

# Table of Contents

# *Introduction*

## Why Center A Bible Study Around A Fictional Character?

*T*he Elsie Dinsmore novels, written by Miss Martha Finley and originally published in 1868, tell the captivating story of the life and spiritual commitment of a young girl named Elsie Dinsmore growing up in the southern United States. On the surface, the Elsie books are delightful fictional stories that entertain and surprise us. Yet anyone who has read these books and experienced the character of Elsie Dinsmore can see that there is far more to be gleaned than just entertainment. There is something different about Elsie Dinsmore.

Even though Elsie is a fictional character born in Miss Finley's imagination, we find in this charming, young heroine an extraordinary faith in Jesus Christ and a passionate determination to apply the Word of God in her everyday life. Tested in ways almost unimaginable to us — through the loss of her mother, years of separation from her father, the rejection of her grandparents, and constant harassment from other children in the family — Elsie nonetheless manages to confront her circumstances with amazing grace. Readers cannot help but desire to have the same strength that empowers Elsie.

But what is the source of Elsie's strength? What enables her to consistently meet the selfishness of others with servanthood, or their hatred with love?

The answer is simple: *all of Elsie's virtue flows from one source — the Holy Spirit born in her through a childlike love for Jesus.* Elsie Dinsmore had one heart-choice settled — she loved God more than anything or anyone else. And that love permeated every part of her being.

*To become like Jesus was the goal of Elsie's life!* This explains why Elsie always wanted to show love to others—even those who mistreated her. Her response to the difficulties in her life seems to echo the words of Paul the apostle: "[In] all these things we are more than conquerors through him who loved us. For I am convinced that neither death nor life, neither angels nor demons, neither the present nor the future, nor any powers, neither height nor depth, nor anything else in all creation, will be able to separate us from the love of God that is in Christ Jesus our Lord" (Romans 8:37–39).

The *A Life of Faith: Elsie Dinsmore*™ series clearly demonstrates that a life of faith arising from a genuine love for Jesus will yield an abundance of love, joy, peace, patience, kindness, goodness, faithfulness, gentleness and self-control — the fruit of God's Holy Spirit as given in Galatians 5:22–23.

## First Things First

$\mathcal{I}$n order to have the fruit of the Holy Spirit, we must first have the Holy Spirit living inside our hearts. When we accept Jesus Christ as our Lord and Savior and commit our lives to Him, His Holy Spirit comes to dwell in our hearts.

If you have not yet accepted Jesus as your Lord and Savior, you can do so right now. It is as simple as saying a prayer to God and believing in the Lord with all of your heart. You can say it in your own words, or you can pray the following simple prayer, either alone or with another Christian:

*Dear Heavenly Father, I know that I am a sinner and have often done things that are wrong. I am sorry for my sins and I pray that You will forgive me for all of them. I accept the free gift of Jesus' death on the Cross in my place. I believe that Jesus died for my sins and was raised from the dead. I invite You and Your Holy Spirit to come live inside my heart. I give my life to You right now, and I ask that from this day forth, You would help me to follow You, to love You more and more, and to get to know You better. Amen.*

If you prayed to accept Jesus, *welcome to the family of God!* Now you can look forward to a wonderful relationship with the *living* God! Tell someone else (preferably another Christian) about the commitment you just made to the Lord, and if that someone else is not your parent, then you should also tell your mother or father or guardian.

## The Fruit of the Holy Spirit

$\mathcal{T}$he frost had disappeared by the time Elsie was dressed. As she did each morning, she settled into her little, rosewood rocking chair — so prized because it was a gift from her father — to read her Bible and talk to Jesus, her beloved Savior and Friend. She enjoyed this time with the Lord immensely. She began by asking the Lord to open her heart and mind to the Scriptures; then she read and reflected on a passage and memorized a verse from the passage she had read. Finally, she knelt to say her morning prayers and asked the Lord to grant her the "fruit of the Spirit" of which Paul spoke in the fifth chapter of the book of Galatians — "love, joy, peace, patience, kindness, goodness, faithfulness, gentleness and self-control."

— *Elsie's Impossible Choice*, pages 3–4

Elsie Dinsmore, from a very young age, made it a habit to spend time with the Lord every day. Jesus Christ was the love of her life, and her relationship with Him was always her chief priority. She would read the Bible and pray, and her daily prayer was that the Lord would help her walk in the "fruit of the Spirit." Galatians 5:22–23 tells us that the fruit of the Spirit is love, joy, peace, patience, kindness, goodness, faithfulness, gentleness and self-control.

When you became a Christian, the Holy Spirit (God's Spirit) came to live inside of you. When that happened, God sowed the seeds of the fruit of the Holy Spirit in the garden of your heart. They are not seeds that you had to plant—the Lord planted them for you.

 **If you are a Christian, the fruit of the Holy Spirit is growing in you!**

If you take a closer look at Galatians 5:22–23, you will see that it tells us that love, joy, peace, patience, kindness, goodness, faithfulness, gentleness, and self-control are fruit *of the Spirit*—they are not fruit *of us*. God Himself (through His Holy Spirit) is the One who produces the fruit—not us. This is GREAT NEWS! It means that if God lives in us, and we are faithful and obedient to Him, *He* will cause the seeds He sowed within us to bear this fruit!

There is something else to notice in Galatians 5:22–23. Remember how it says that "the *fruit* of the Spirit is love, joy, peace, patience, kindness, goodness, faithfulness, gentleness and self-control." That is an interesting sentence because it involves a list of several things, but the noun "fruit" is *singular*, as if only one trait or characteristic should follow. With all the items listed, it should read, "The fruit of the Spirit *are . . .*" but it doesn't. It says, the fruit of the Spirit *is . . .* You see, the fruit of the Holy Spirit is really *one gift* with nine different parts or dimensions.

Have you ever seen one of those Russian wooden dolls that you can unscrew and open to find another doll inside? The second doll, too, unscrews and a third doll is in it. Of course, the third doll opens to reveal a fourth, and so on. This is what the fruit of the Holy Spirit is like. Love opens and joy is inside. Joy leads to peace, and peace brings patience, and on through the other traits to self-control.

That's incredible! Everything we need is found in one gift—the Holy Spirit—that we receive when we invite Jesus into our hearts! What we need is to learn how to live in such a way that the fruit of the Spirit can *grow in us* and *flow through us*. That is why we have written this study guide—to teach you how to walk in the fruit of God's Holy Spirit. We will learn it as we examine the life and Christian character of Elsie Dinsmore.

# How to Use This Study Guide

### Before Beginning Your Study

*B*ecause Elsie's Life Lessons is based on plots and sub-plots of the first two books of the *A Life of Faith: Elsie Dinsmore* series, we recommend that you read both Elsie's Endless Wait and Elsie's Impossible Choice prior to beginning this study. For convenience, we will quote brief portions from those two Elsie novels. But this, by no means, can substitute for being familiar with the characters and story lines. And you will enjoy knowing Elsie more fully.

### Studying Elsie's Life Lessons

*U*nlike the novels from the *A Life of Faith: Elsie Dinsmore* series, this study guide is not designed for you to sit down and read cover to cover. The object of our study is to grow in God's ways and to become more like Jesus. This takes time. We hope that you will progress through *Elsie's Life Lessons* gradually, with careful thought and prayer.

As you embark on *Elsie's Life Lessons*, remember that your goal is not to finish the study quickly, but to "be transformed by the renewing of your mind," as Romans 12:2 encourages us. Each chapter in this study guide has five lessons. *Do not attempt to complete a whole chapter in one day or at one time.* Instead, do each lesson slowly, one at a time. Allow its truths to inspire your thoughts, penetrate your heart, and influence your actions before you move on. It's important not to skip any of the learning activities. We have purposefully chosen each question and assignment to help you understand and apply God's truths to your life.

**Throughout this course, you will find that the only way for you to become more like Jesus is to grow in your love for Him.**

As you read and write, remember that what you're doing is about much more than what is seen and written on paper. *Expect to experience God.* With each question and assignment, look for Him and listen to what He is personally saying to you. If you get stuck or need help understanding something, do not be reluctant to ask your parents, your youth leader, or a Christian friend. God often speaks to us through other people. Also, we have intentionally included some words in this study guide that will be a challenge for you. *Keep a dictionary handy so that you can learn the meanings of new words!*

This is *your* book. Be open and honest with your answers. Feel free to write in the margins, to jot down additional ideas, and to make a note of questions that may come to mind. Use additional sheets of paper if you find that you need more room to write.

It is very important that you seek to *apply* the principles you will learn in this study guide to your everyday life. To help you, we have included some symbols at the end of each chapter to remind you to *stop and digest what you have learned.*

When you see this symbol, pause and look back over the chapter. Ask the Holy Spirit to show you the most important things He wants you to remember. Put a star beside those truths. Then, in your own words, summarize what He showed you.

When you see this symbol, rewrite your thoughts as a prayer, asking God to help you grow and apply the truths He's taught you throughout the chapter.

## Scripture Memory: From God's Heart to Yours

God wrote His Word — the Bible — to *you*, like a letter from a Beloved Friend. Verse by verse, page by page, God pours out His heart to us. Unlike any other book, the Bible is very personal; and, of course, it's perfect and complete truth. God's Word, then, is far more important to us than any note a friend could send. We're told that "the grass withers and the flowers fall, but the Word of our God stands forever" (Isaiah 40:8). We want to spend all the days of our lives reading His Word, thinking about it, and even learning it by heart.

**We use the phrase "to learn something by heart" when we memorize it because *our hearts and minds are connected.* What we choose to think about will affect our hearts for better or worse.**

In 2 Corinthians 10:5, the Holy Spirit counsels us to "take captive every thought to make it obedient to Christ." If our thoughts are obedient, if they agree with God's thoughts, our hearts, too, will be obedient. The Bible says that *we are transformed into the nature of Jesus when we renew our minds with God's Word* (Romans 12:2). Scripture memory is very important! It is not just learning. In a way, it's like eating. As we fill ourselves with God's Word, we build strong and healthy lives.

For those reasons, we've included learning Scripture "by heart" in *Elsie's Life Lessons*.

This large heart symbol will mark the memory verse for each chapter. Work on memorizing the verse before, during and after you read the chapter.

This small heart symbol will mark the memory verse for the entire study guide, Galatians 5:22–23. Work on memorizing it and testing yourself on how well you remember it throughout all of *Elsie's Life Lessons*.

Some of the memory verses will be short and fairly easy to memorize; others will be more difficult. But TAKE YOUR TIME. Scripture memory is well worth the investment of time you put into it!

At the end of this book, we have included Scripture Memory Cards that you can use as a help. Here are some suggestions for how to use them:

❖ Remove the cards from the back of this book and use them as flash cards.

❖ Study one card at a time.

❖ Read the verse and think about the meaning. Make sure you understand all the words in the text. Think about how it applies to you. Ask others (such as your parents or youth leader or a Christian friend) what they think God is saying in the verse.

❖ Make a sign with the verse written on it and hang it in full view where you spend time or will see it each day—near your bed, at your desk, on the refrigerator, or elsewhere.

❖ Carry the verse card with you. Recite the verse out loud several times throughout the day. Do this while riding in the car, waiting in line, during breaks at school, etc.

❖ Quiz yourself until you can recite the verse without looking.

❖ Recite the verse to a parent or friend until you get it perfect.

❖ Wait until one verse is committed to memory before moving on to the next.

❖ With each new verse you study, do not neglect the ones you've already memorized. Continue reciting and quizzing yourself on each verse you learned.

❖ Think about these verses as you speak, act, and make decisions. Ask God to help you to live these truths in everything you do.

❖ If you can, find someone (a parent or friend) who will memorize verses along with you. Then you can test each other!

Most of all, remember this: *God wants to personally speak to you through His Word.* Though the verses may come from a book that all the world can read, it's as if God is confiding the secrets of His heart to you — His precious child and friend. Ask Him, "What do You want me to learn from this today, Lord?" And expect an answer. He will show you. Of course, you can share these secrets. But treasure them and never forget that they're special . . . like letters from a Friend.

## Last Words

𝒪ur hope for you, as you learn God's Word and discover more about walking in the fruit of the Holy Spirit through *Elsie's Life Lessons*, is that you will enjoy this study and enjoy being close to God. *Invest in your relationship with the Lord as you would with your dearest friend.* You'll find that the more time you spend getting to know Him, the more you will love Him and desire a closer relationship with Him. Give Jesus your whole heart, your whole mind, and full access to every nook and cranny of your soul. Desire for His Spirit to envelop yours, and expect Him to guide and sustain your life. Look for Him. Listen for Him. Remind yourself that He's everywhere you go, involved in everything that you do. Imagine: The Creator of the whole universe is walking by your side like a faithful Companion. Wow!

Now, if you are ready to begin, take some time to memorize Galatians 5:22–23, the key verse for this entire study guide. Be sure you have memorized it "by heart" before moving on to the first chapter. Once you have memorized it, we will study each part of the fruit of the Spirit, one at a time. *Elsie's Life Lessons* will bring you a great harvest of life in the Spirit.

*But the fruit of the Spirit is love, joy, peace, patience, kindness, goodness, faithfulness, gentleness and self-control.*

GALATIANS 5:22–23

# CHAPTER

## Walking in Love

# *Walking in Love*

**by heart**

*L*ove is patient, love is kind. It does not envy, it does not boast, it is not proud. It is not rude, it is not self-seeking, it is not easily angered, it keeps no record of wrongs. Love does not delight in evil but rejoices with the truth. It always protects, always trusts, always hopes, always perseveres. Love never fails.
— 1 CORINTHIANS 13:4–8

## God's Love Makes the Difference

*E*lsie opened her book to the fifty-third chapter of Isaiah, and when her father had read the verses to her, she asked for the twenty-third chapter of Luke. As Horace read, in his fine, clear voice, Elsie closed her eyes and a look of peace seemed to fill her face.

When he finished, Horace asked, "What made you choose this chapter, my dear?"

"Because it is all about Jesus and tells us how patiently He bore sorrow and suffering. I want so much to be like Him, Papa. To hear about Him makes it easier for me to forgive and be patient, just as He forgave."

"You're thinking about Arthur," Horace observed accurately. "I will find it very hard to forgive him. I know all about what happened and how badly he has treated you." Then he recounted to her everything that had occurred that evening.

Tears welled in Elsie's eyes and tumbled down her cheeks. "I don't understand," she said, "why Arthur hates me so. I've always tried to be kind to him. I had to tell on him once — that time when he blamed Jim for breaking Grandpa's watch. But that was the only time."

Horace put a comforting arm around her. "You no longer have to worry about him, Elsie. He is being sent away to boarding school, so he will have no more opportunities to hurt you."

Elsie stiffened. "Boarding school?" she said with a sharp little cry. "Oh, Papa, that's terrible! I can't think of anything worse than being sent away and having to live with strangers. Can't you ask Grandpa to forgive him this time? Must he be sent away?"

Elsie's reaction surprised Horace, and he tried to reassure her: "It's really for his own good, dear . . . ."

Horace stayed while Elsie prayed, and he listened carefully to her words. To his amazement, much of what Elsie said concerned Arthur. She asked her heavenly Father to forgive the boy and guide him through the trials ahead. She asked Him to help Arthur conquer his evil ways. And she asked that Arthur should come to know God's love in his heart.

"Will I never understand my child?" Horace asked himself as he left her room a few moments later. "How can she be so forgiving, when I feel only rage? What is this difference between us?"

— *Elsie's Impossible Choice*, pages 78–80

"What is this difference between us?" Elsie's father, Horace, asked himself. Truly, what was the difference? How could Elsie, a mere child, be more giving and more forgiving than her father, a full-grown man of high moral character? How could Elsie be more compassionate and kind? More patient, especially since she lived at the mercy of those who seemed to have no mercy for her?

The difference was that, as a Christian, Elsie had God's Holy Spirit living inside her.

 **The Holy Spirit enabled Elsie to love others with God's love, even when they did not love her.**

Take a moment to think about love and write down your own definition for it. Be as specific as possible.

Most people think that love is the nice, warm feeling you feel when you have a very strong liking for someone or something. But how does the Bible define love? What is *God's* definition of love?

The answer to that question is in 1 Corinthians 13:4–8. Look again at our memory verse for this chapter and think about the Bible's description of love:

"Love is patient, love is kind. It does not envy, it does not boast, it is not proud. It is not rude, it is not self-seeking, it is not easily angered, it keeps no record of wrongs. Love does not delight in evil but rejoices with the truth. It always protects, always trusts, always hopes, always perseveres. Love never fails."

From that definition, we can see that *love means a whole lot more than a nice, warm feeling!* In fact, if you look carefully at the definition again, you will see that a nice, warm feeling is not even mentioned!

To understand more about what love is, let's look at what love *isn't*. In the space below, across from the list of love's virtues from 1 Corinthians 13, write the opposite quality or behavior for each one.

| Love Is ... | Love Is Not ... |
| --- | --- |
| patient | impatient |
| kind | |
| not envious | |
| not boastful | |
| not proud | |
| not rude | |
| not selfish | |
| not easily angered | |
| doesn't record wrongs | |
| rejoices in truth | |
| protects | |
| trusts | |
| hopes | |
| perseveres | |
| never fails | |

If you're like most people, in the list of opposites you no doubt saw a number of qualities or behaviors that you struggle with in your relationships with your parents, brothers and sisters, teachers, classmates, friends, and others.

List below some of the relationships where you find it hard to love according to the prior definition. Next to each relationship, list your feelings or behaviors that fall in the "Love Is Not" category (for example, my younger brother—impatience).

**Contrary to popular belief, love—God's definition of love—has everything to do with how we treat others and little to do with how we feel.**

Jesus says, "But I tell you who hear me: Love your *enemies*, do good to those *who hate you*, bless those *who curse you*, pray for those *who mistreat you*" (Luke 6:27). Clearly, Jesus wants us to love those who we do not feel like loving!

In the above verse of Scripture, did you notice the action words "do good," "bless," and "pray for?" From these words, we see two things. Love involves *action*. Love also involves making *choices*—*hard* choices and *heart* choices.

What do you think it means to *choose* to love someone?

When we read about Elsie in *Elsie's Endless Wait*, we see that she often made the *choice* to love the people in her life even when it was very difficult. Can you recall some of the things Elsie *did* do because of love, as well as some of the things she *didn't* do because of love? We'll get you started, but see if you can add to this list. (Remember, you're not in a race. It's okay to stop and think and move slowly through this study. Learning *Elsie's Life Lessons* takes time.)

## Things Elsie Did Do

Elsie bought a boat for Arthur as a gift.
Elsie told the truth on Jim's behalf.

## Things Elsie Didn't Do

Elsie did not get even with Arthur for getting her in trouble with Miss Day.

Have you ever *chosen* to love when it was really hard for you? Perhaps you were hurt by someone, or treated unfairly like Elsie. Maybe you didn't like the way someone looked or perhaps you just didn't *feel* like loving them. Stop to think about one of those times. Write down what you *felt* like doing, and then write down how you *chose* to love instead.

What happened when you chose to love in that circumstance? What was the result?

What do you imagine could have happened if you hadn't chosen to love in that situation?

It would be nice if all of us chose to love all the time and never reacted in impatience or anger or did what we *felt* like doing when we were wronged or hurt by another person. The truth is that no one is perfect, and most of us have, at one time or another, reacted to others by doing what we felt like doing instead of *choosing* to love God's way. But the good news is that God still loves us! And when our love fails, His love never does.

 **God never runs out of love, and His love inside of us can help us choose to respond to others in a loving way even when our human emotions might want us to do otherwise.**

The Bible declares, "If we love one another, God lives in us and *his love* is made complete in us" (1 John 4:12).

# First Love

> "Do you love Jesus, Papa?"
>
> This question greatly concerned Elsie, but instead of answering her, Horace asked, "Do you, Elsie?"
>
> "Oh, yes, sir! Very much. I love Him even better than I love you, my own dear father."
>
> He searched her little face. "How do you know that?" he wondered.
>
> "Just as I know I love you," she responded with evident surprise. "I love to talk of Jesus. I love to tell Him all my troubles, and ask Him to forgive my sins and make me holy. It means so much to know that He loves me and always will, even if no one else does."
>
> —*Elsie's Endless Wait*, pages 165

One thing we know about Elsie is that she loved Jesus with all of her heart. Jesus was, after all, her father when she had no father, her best friend when she had no one but Aunt Chloe to love her, her comforter in times of trouble, and her beloved Savior and Redeemer. Elsie loved Jesus *best*—even more than she loved her father (which was a lot)!

Describe your feelings about Jesus—what He means to you and how you know that you love Him.

Jesus told us in Matthew 22:37–38 that the first and greatest commandment was to love the Lord your God with all your heart and with all your soul and with all your mind.

 **Our Christian walk is about a love relationship with the Lord!**

When you love others, you want to get to know them better and be with them as much as you can, and the same is true for our relationship with Jesus. If we love Jesus, we will spend time getting to know Him by reading His Word. We will talk to Him in prayer. We will talk about Him with other believers. We will want to share our joys and our troubles with Him. We will worship Him with songs of praise and adoration. And we will show Him our love in many other ways.

But the Bible tells us something else very important that we can do to show Jesus that we love Him. Elsie explains what it is to Horace in the following passage.

> When Elsie was at last wrapped in her covers, [Horace] asked, "Why did you pray that I might love Jesus?"
>
> "Because I want you to be happy, and I want you to go to heaven, Papa."
>
> "And what makes you think I don't love Him?"
>
> "Don't be angry, Papa, but you know what Jesus says: 'Whoever has my commands and obeys them, he is the one who loves me.'"
>
> —*Elsie's Endless Wait*, page 194

As Elsie pointed out to her father, Jesus said, "Whoever has my commands and obeys them, he is the one who loves me" (John 14:21). In another verse, 1 John 5:3, Jesus tells us something similar. He says, "This is love for God: to obey his commands."

Obedience, commands . . . those don't sound like words of love. But there is a connection between obedience and love. Read John 14:21 and 1 John 5:3 again and then describe the connection between obedience and love.

How then do we show our love to God?

How then do you show your love to your parents?

# The Word of God

"I must go now and let you learn your lesson," Rose said. "But perhaps you'd like to come to my room in the mornings and evenings and read your Bible to me."

"Oh, yes, ma'am," Elsie exclaimed, and her eyes sparkled with delight. "I love reading the Bible best of anything! Aunt Chloe has always taught me that I must 'hide the Word in my heart.'"

"And have you memorized all of your verses by heart?" Rose inquired.

"Not all of them," Elsie said honestly. "But I've memorized many beautiful passages."

"Can you recite something for me?" Rose asked, for she could see that their discussion of God's Word greatly cheered the child.

Elsie thought for a few moments, then said: "Yes, ma'am. These verses from Colossians are some of my favorites." She quoted carefully: "'Therefore, as God's chosen people, holy and dearly loved, clothe yourselves with compassion, kindness, humility, gentleness and patience. Bear with each other and forgive whatever grievances you may have against one another. Forgive as the Lord forgave you. And over all these virtues put on love, which binds them all together in perfect unity.'"

"That is excellent, Elsie!" Rose said, smiling brightly. "And why do you like those verses?"

"Because they're so clear to me, Miss Allison. I sometimes have trouble understanding what I read in the Scriptures."

"Then perhaps I can help you. If you like, we can study God's Word together," Rose said.

"Oh, how kind you are," Elsie replied happily. "I would like that very much."

—*Elsie's Endless Wait*, pages 15–16

As we read previously, Jesus said, "This is love for God: to obey his commands" (1 John 5:3). How, though, can we obey God if we don't *know* His commands? To know Jesus, we must know — *and love* — His Word. If Jesus is our first love, the Bible will be the first thing we reach for. In fact, we won't be able to live without it!

Sometimes people read the Bible as if it is a discipline or a chore. But how did Elsie feel about the Word of God? In the passage above, Elsie said she loved reading the Bible "best of anything!" Just hearing God's words brought her comfort.

**With Jesus as her first love, Elsie wanted to know everything He ever said. She based her hope on His promises, not on circumstances or the words of others. Because she loved and trusted Him, she loved and trusted in His Word.**

And she obeyed Him. Because she knew what He commanded, she knew what He expected from her. She obeyed God's Word out of love—and she loved to obey it!

Long before the *Elsie Dinsmore* series was written, there was someone else who wrote of his love for God's Word. In Psalm 119:72, King David said: "The law from your mouth is more precious to me than thousands of pieces of silver and gold." And in Psalm 119:127–129 he added, "Because I love your commands more than gold, more than pure gold, and because I consider all your precepts right, I hate every wrong path. Your statutes are wonderful; therefore I obey them." *Loving God means loving and obeying His Word!*

Why do you think reading the Bible is different from reading any other book?

Hebrews 4:12 tells us that "the word of God is *living and active.* Sharper than any double-edged sword, it penetrates even to dividing soul and spirit, joints and marrow; *it judges the thoughts and attitudes of the heart.*"

In what way does the Bible judge the thoughts and attitudes of your heart?

Read these other comments that David made about the Word of God and underline the words that indicate the benefit that comes from reading the Bible:

Psalm 119:9–11  "How can a young man keep his way pure? By living according to your word. I seek you with all my heart; do not let me stray from your commands. I have hidden your word in my heart that I might not sin against you."

Psalm 119:98–99  "Your commands make me wiser than my enemies, for they are ever with me. I have more insight than all my teachers, for I meditate on your statutes."

Psalm 119:105  "Your word is a lamp to my feet and a light for my path."

Do you remember what Horace said about Elsie and her constant interest in the Word of God? "My child finds *wisdom* in the Bible," he said. Horace went on to say that he was "amazed at how often that book seems to *protect her from evil influences*" (see *Elsie's Impossible Choice*, page 31). The Bible teaches us principles that will guide and protect us our whole lives long!

Summarize in your own words the benefits of reading the Word of God (some are found in the verses and statements by Horace above, but also include in your list other benefits that you can think of):

You can see that reading the Bible involves much more than information entering our minds. It's God Himself speaking to us, protecting us, touching our spirits, examining and changing our minds, our hearts, and every area of our lives!

The good news is that even if you don't like to read, even if you find reading boring, the Bible is different! *It is about relationship with God! It's like going over to your best friend's house and having a special, private conversation.* The Word of God is alive — it's living and active! When you curl up in your most comfortable chair to read the Bible, expect to hear and experience God!

# Loving Others

*T*he young woman gazed at the portrait admiringly, then she turned to Elsie in puzzlement. "I don't understand," Rose said. "Are you not the sister of Enna and the other children? Is Mrs. Dinsmore not your mother?"

"She is their mother, but not mine," Elsie replied. "My father, Horace Dinsmore, Jr., is their brother, so all the other children are my aunts and uncles."

"Indeed," Rose mused. "And your father is away, isn't he?"

"Yes, ma'am. He's in Europe. He has been away since before I was born, and I've never seen him. Oh, I do wish he'd come home! I want to see him so much! Do you think he would love me, Miss Allison? Do you think he would put me on his knee and hug me the way Grandpa hugs Enna?"

"I'm sure he would, my dear. How could he help loving his own little girl?" said Rose, and she gently kissed Elsie's cheek.

— *Elsie's Endless Wait*, page 15

Reading of Elsie's loneliness reminds us how much we need love. "It is not good for man to be alone," God said when He created us (Genesis 2:18). According to *His* design, we were meant to need each other. Elsie later told her father, "I used to feel so lonely sometimes, Papa, that I thought my heart would really break. I think I would have died if I had not had Jesus to love me" (*Elsie's Endless Wait*, page 183). Truly, our need for love is great!

Every day of our lives, there are numerous things we need from others — food, shelter, safety, fair treatment, and so on. Most of all, we need *love*, and that includes many things, such as respect, kindness, understanding, acceptance, and being valued as a unique individual with our strengths appreciated and our weaknesses overlooked. We'd like forgiveness when we fail, and grace when we come close to failing. And we have many other needs too.

Recall a typical day in your life. Beginning when you wake up in the morning, until you go to bed at night, what are some of the things you need from the people who share your life?

Jesus knew what He was saying when He summarized all of the Law and the Prophets in two simple commands: "*Love* the Lord your God with all your heart and with all your soul and with all your mind," and "*Love* your neighbor as yourself" (Matthew 22:37–39). God not only created us to depend on love, but He established a world where everything revolves around it.

It may seem hard to believe that we wouldn't naturally know what love is, especially since we have such tremendous need of it. But, sadly, our ideas about love are often not right.

Where do most people get their ideas of what love is?

Where does true love come from?

First John 4:16 tells us that "God is love." This helps us understand why the fruit of the Holy Spirit is love. When our hearts are filled with love for the Lord—as Elsie's was—His Spirit within us overflows with love for others. When we find it difficult to love, turning our hearts toward our Savior miraculously gives us what we need to extend love to others in every circumstance. That is why Elsie's love was so amazing—*she had an extraordinary ability to love because she let Jesus love others through her!*

Romans 12:10 gives us a way to love. It says, "Honor others above yourselves." Philippians 2:3 says nearly the same thing: "Do nothing out of selfish ambition or vain conceit, but in humility *consider others better than yourself.*"

With her possessions, how did Elsie consider others above herself?

With your possessions, how can you consider others above yourself?

Go back to the list you wrote on the previous page about your typical day. Think of the many people in your life. Let's turn the focus from what we need, instead, to what we can *give* to make others feel loved. You can gather ideas from the list of your own needs. Remember what Jesus said — "Love your neighbor as yourself."

In the space below, list some key people in your life and fill in the attitudes you could have and the actions you could do to make that person feel loved.

| Name | Attitudes | Actions |
| --- | --- | --- |
| My teacher, Miss Day | Respectful | Obedience and good classroom behavior |

 Because Elsie loved God, she was able to love even those who treated her cruelly. Her love didn't depend on their actions. Her love depended on God.

Jesus declared, "By this will all men know you are my disciples, if you love one another" (John 13:35). We count on the fruit of God's Holy Spirit to put love in our hearts for one another, because we cannot truly love others without His help. Do you remember God's definition of love from 1 Corinthians 13:4–8? If so, write it here.

# Loving Our Enemies

Silenced, Arthur tiptoed across the room and crept up behind Elsie. Taking a feather from his pocket, he tickled it at the back of her neck. She jumped in surprise, then pleaded with Arthur to stop.

"But it pleases me to bother you," Arthur said, and he tickled her once more.

With all the persuasion she could muster, Elsie asked him again, "Please leave me alone, or I'll never get this problem done."

"All this time on one little problem?" Arthur replied with a sneering laugh. "You ought to be ashamed, Elsie Dinsmore. Why, I could have done it a half a dozen times before now."

"Well, I've been over it and over it," Elsie said sadly, "and there are still two numbers that won't come out right."

"How do you know they're not right, little miss?" Arthur asked, grabbing at her curls as he spoke.

"Please don't pull my hair!" she cried . . . . Elsie tried to turn her attention to her geography book, but Arthur would not stop his persecutions. He tickled her, pulled at her hair, flipped the book out of her hands, and kept up his incessant chatter and questions. On the verge of tears, Elsie begged him once again to leave her to her lessons . . . . But Arthur stood over her as she wrote, criticizing every letter she made. At last, he jogged her elbow, and all the ink in her pen dropped onto the paper, making a large black blot. It was too much, and Elsie burst into tears. "Now I won't get to ride to the fair! Miss Day will never let me go! And I wanted so much to see the beautiful flowers. . . ."

> The hour was up, and Miss Day returned . . . . Noting the two incorrect numbers in Elsie's arithmetic problem, Miss Day put down the girl's slate and opened the copybook. "You careless, disobedient child!" she shouted. "Didn't I tell you not to blot your book? There will be no ride for you today. You have failed in everything."
>
> — *Elsie's Endless Wait*, pages 5–8

Through no fault of her own, Elsie had many "enemies." Even though she faithfully returned love for insult and injury, her life at Roselands was full of people who constantly provoked her. However, this did not change the Word of God for Elsie. It did not alter the Lord's expectations that demanded she walk in love. In fact, if you recall, in the above situation, *Elsie's response was to examine her own heart and repent to her teacher for her anger and impatience* — even though she was treated unjustly! Wow! What humility! How did she do it?

**Elsie had such love for her Savior that she wanted to be like Him in *every way*, including loving and forgiving those who mistreated her.**

Apart from God, how would we naturally treat our enemies?

Jesus tells us, "Do to others as you would have them do to you" (Luke 6:31). And in Matthew 5:43–44, He says, "You have heard that it was said, 'Love your neighbor and hate your enemy.' But I tell you: *Love your enemies and pray for those who persecute you.*"

An "enemy" comes in all different shapes and sizes. Though we might not come right out and call someone an enemy, we associate the word with a person we're at odds with, someone who has hurt us and has not asked for our pardon. Perhaps the person has always been mean towards us. Or perhaps the person is a friend we have loved, but who has hurt us without meaning to. An enemy might be someone we know at a distance, or someone we see every day.

Jesus asks us, "If you love those who love you, what credit is that to you? Even 'sinners' love those who love them. And if you do good to those who are good to you, what credit is that to you? Even 'sinners' do that. And if you lend to those from whom you expect repayment, what credit is that to you? Even 'sinners' lend to 'sinners,' expecting to be repaid in full. *But love your enemies,*" Jesus says again. "Do good to them, and lend to them without expecting to get anything back" (Luke 6:32–35). Jesus continues, "Then your reward will be great, and you will be sons of the Most High, *because he is kind to the ungrateful and wicked.* Be merciful, just as your Father is merciful" (v. 36).

What type of people do you tend to avoid? In other words, when you are honest with yourself, what type of people do you have trouble being kind and considerate toward?

What acts of service or kind gestures do you do for your friends that, perhaps, you could do for those you mentioned?

We know that the kind of love Jesus wants us to have is not self-seeking. Love desires us to uplift others solely for *their* welfare. Everyone needs love, especially the "unlovely" or the unsaved.

*Love is not about receiving. Real love is about giving.* It flows from a pure and tender heart (one that is free of resentment, selfish motives, and other things that harden the heart) and a love for God that wants to see Him honored above all else. That's the kind of love we see given by Elsie! *Elsie could love like that because she trusted that she was secure in God's love and knew that loving people His way would bring Him glory.* She knew that opportunities to love where it was not expected or deserved—such as when she bought Arthur the boat he wanted—were *golden opportunities* presented to her by God.

Can you think of any "golden opportunities" to love that God has placed in your life right now? If so, list them here.

**Remember, it is God's love in us that gives us the power to love others beyond our human ability. God's love allows us to love people even after we have reached our human limits and run out of love.**

No wonder Elsie was able to love Arthur, Enna, Miss Day, her stepmother, and others. God's love in her made the difference, and God's love in YOU can make the difference too!

Look back over this chapter. Ask the Holy Spirit to show you the most important things He wants you to remember. Put a star beside those truths and, in your own words, summarize below what He showed you.

Rewrite your thoughts as a prayer, asking God to help you grow and apply the truths He's taught you throughout the chapter.

Write out the memory verse for this chapter:

Write out Galatians 5:22–23, the memory verse for our entire study guide:

# CHAPTER

**2**

## *Walking in Joy*

# Walking In Joy

*by heart*

*C*onsider it pure joy, my brothers, whenever you face trials of many kinds, because you know that the testing of your faith develops perseverance. Perseverance must finish its work so that you may be mature and complete, not lacking anything.
—JAMES 1:2–4

## The Joy of Loving Jesus

*A*s there was no school and her father was called into a business discussion, Elsie retreated to the garden to read her Bible. She had been alone there for some time when she heard someone approaching. It was Edward Travilla.

He saw how intent she looked, and sitting beside her, he glanced at the book she held.

"What can you be reading that affects you so?" he asked.

"Oh, Mr. Travilla, doesn't it make your heart ache to read how our dear Savior was so abused, and then to know it was all because of our sins. Isn't it wonderful to know that we can be saved from the penalty for our sins, and be His friend now, and someday go to heaven?"

Her ideas intrigued him. "Really, Elsie," he said, "you are quite right, but aren't such ideas very serious for a young girl like you?"

"Mr. Travilla," she exclaimed. "These ideas bring me such peace and joy. When I read my Bible like this, I sometimes feel as if Jesus were sitting here beside me, just as you are."

"Can a person really be that close to God?" he asked half-jokingly.

"Oh yes, sir. Our dear Savior wants all His children to draw near to Him. You only have to *want* to spend time with Him, for He is always ready and waiting with His love," she replied.

— *Elsie's Endless Wait*, pages 195–196

*A*s can be seen in the passage on the previous page, Elsie Dinsmore knew what it was to walk in the fruit of joy. Simply put, *Elsie was in love—in love with Jesus!* Because He was the love of her life, she lived each day filled with inner joy.

The dictionary defines "joy" as a feeling or state of great delight, keen pleasure, or happiness. Like love, joy may cause happy, elated feelings. But the joy born of the Holy Spirit—the fruit of joy—is much more than that. It flows from a deep, abiding trust in the security of God's love. It's like what a nursing baby feels in the arms of his or her mother. Infants may become tired, hungry, or wet, and may cry, but the nearness of the mother assures them that all is well. They have the joy of secure love!

Look again at the above passage and notice from the tone of Elsie's comments how warm and personal Elsie's relationship with Jesus was. Elsie found peace, joy, and great delight in her relationship with Him. She trusted so much in the security of His love that the fruit of joy was the result. Psalm 33:21 says, "In Him our hearts *rejoice*, for we *trust* in his holy name." When love trusts, joy results!

How would you describe your relationship with Jesus? Do you trust in the security of His love?

How does a person find the joy that Elsie did? Psalm 16:11 gives us a clue. In it, David says to God, "You have made known to me the path of life; you will fill me with joy *in your presence*." In the King James Version, that verse reads, "In your presence there is fullness of joy." Think about that. *Fullness* of joy is found in the presence of the Lord!

 **Clearly, one of Elsie's "secrets" to walking in the fruit of the Spirit was that she LOVED to spend time with the Lord.**

Do you *love* to spend time with the Lord? Why or why not?

The joy of loving Jesus, and being loved by Him, consumed Elsie. We constantly see her praying, reading her Bible, worshiping the Lord, and contemplating the things of God. Adelaide said about Elsie, "She is forever reading her Bible" (see *Elsie's Endless Wait*, page 192). That's because in reading it, Elsie found great joy. No wonder she spent so much of her time reading, studying, learning, and memorizing Scripture!

Look up the following Scriptures in your Bible. Write out each of the verses and see if they seem to echo Elsie's feelings about the Word of God:

Psalm 19:8 –

Psalm 119:14 –

Psalm 119:111 –

What things, if any, could you cut out or reorganize in your life in order to spend more time with the Lord and in the Word of God?

# Joy In Suffering

True, Adelaide often treated Elsie affectionately, but they were far apart in age and Adelaide had little time to spend with her young niece. Lora, who had a strong sense of justice, occasionally intervened and took Elsie's side when she was unfairly accused. But none of the Dinsmores seemed to really care for her, and Elsie was often lonely and sad. Her grandfather, Horace Dinsmore, Sr., treated her with complete neglect and usually spoke of her as "old Grayson's grandchild." Mrs. Dinsmore genuinely disliked her, as the child of the stepson for whom she had no fondness and as a future rival to her own daughters. The younger children, following the example of their parents, usually neglected Elsie and sometimes mistreated her. Miss Day, knowing that there was no danger her employers would object, vented on Elsie the spite she dared not show her other pupils. Again and again, Elsie was made to give up her playthings to Enna, and sometimes to Arthur and Walter. This treatment often caused Elsie to struggle with her temper; had she possessed less of a meek and gentle spirit, her life might have been wretched indeed.

But in spite of it all, Elsie was the happiest person in the family, for she had peace in her heart and felt the joy which the Savior gives to His own. She constantly took her sorrows and troubles to Him, and the coldness and neglect of the others only drove her closer to her Heavenly Friend. While she had His love, she could not be unhappy, and her trials seemed to make her naturally amiable character even more lovely.

— *Elsie's Endless Wait*, pages 30–31

The Bible tells us to *"be joyful always*; pray continually; give thanks in *all* circumstances, for this is God's will for you in Christ Jesus" (1 Thessalonians 5:16–18). To this, you may ask, "*Always* joyful? Thankful in *all* circumstances? But how?"

**True joy does not depend on our circumstances or the people around us.**

That is what we see in Elsie's life. The excerpt above says "*But in spite of it all*, Elsie was the happiest person in the family." Neglect, mistreatment, rejection, jealousy — in spite of them all, Elsie had joy. Elsie's joy in loving Jesus is what carried her through trial after trial.

In Philippians 4:12, the apostle Paul said, "I know what it is to be in need, and I know what it is to have plenty. I have learned the secret of being content in any and every situation, whether well fed or hungry, whether living in plenty or in want." What was Paul's secret?

To people that don't know the Lord, it might not make sense that someone like Paul, or Elsie, could possess joy and contentment in difficult circumstances, in suffering, or in tragedy. But from the lives of Paul and Elsie, we can see that it's quite possible to possess the joy of the Lord in such situations.

Joy is not blind to problems or loss. But when we know that God loves us, our joy has the ability to soften our pain or sorrow by helping us continue to hope and trust in God's love. "'For I know the plans I have for you,' declares the Lord, 'plans to prosper you and not to harm you, plans to give you hope and a future'" (Jeremiah 29:11). "All things work for the good of those who love God and are called according to His purpose," we read in Romans 8:28.

Nobody likes to suffer. But is it possible that suffering accomplishes something good in us? If so, what do you think that something good is?

Read the following verse slowly and consider what it promises us. Then go back through it and circle the words "joy," "faith," and "rejoice" wherever you find them:

> In this you greatly rejoice, though now for a little while you may have had to suffer grief in all kinds of trials. These have come so that your faith — of greater worth than gold, which perishes even though refined by fire — may be proved genuine and may result in praise, glory and honor when Jesus Christ is revealed. Though you have not seen him, you love him; and even though you do not see him now, you believe in him and are filled with an inexpressible and glorious joy, for you are receiving the goal of your faith, the salvation of your souls. (1 Peter 1:6–9)

What does that verse tell us that is similar to our memory verse, James 1:2–4?

Are you experiencing anything today that is causing you to suffer? Do you need a little bit of joy? Take a moment now and pray to the Lord. Share your heart with Him and ask Him to fill you with His joy, regardless of your circumstances.

# Keeping Heart

Elsie went to her Bible and read these words: "For it has been granted to you on behalf of Christ not only to believe on Him, but also to suffer for Him . . . ." It was clear to her now that she was suffering for His sake, that her trials had come because she loved Him and would not betray His commands even to please her dear Papa. Her endurance was an act of love, and endure she must, for she could not betray her Savior even though loving Him was not always easy. In God's Word, she found the promise that "the God of all grace, who called you to His eternal glory in Christ, after you have suffered a little while, will Himself restore you . . . ." She cried again, but for the first time in a very long while, her tears came from thankfulness, because she had again found a promise in God's Word to sustain her.

— *Elsie's Impossible Choice*, page 174

The first two books of the *A Life of Faith: Elsie Dinsmore* series are aptly titled *Elsie's Endless Wait* and *Elsie's Impossible Choice*. Sadly, however, *endless* and *impossible* applied to more than just Elsie's "wait" and her "choice." Daily, it seems, Elsie confronted endless impossibilities. Yet never did Elsie *lose heart*. Because she knew and believed God's Word, she could trust in promises like Isaiah 41:10: "So do not fear, for I am with you; do not be dismayed, for I am your God. I will strengthen you and help you; I will uphold you with my righteous right hand."

As we discussed earlier, Elsie loved the Word of God. She not only read the promises she found there, but she *relied* on those promises. As you grow in your knowledge of Scripture, you too will find promises that you will rely on. This is a wonderful benefit of spending time in God's Word.

Do you have a favorite promise from the Word of God? If so, write it out here.

Describe the ways in which you rely on that promise.

Our memory verse, James 1:2–4, tells us that the testing of our faith produces "perseverance." To persevere means to continue or persist at something despite obstacles, opposition, or difficulties. By definition, perseverance is neither easy nor comfortable. Remember the suffering of Elsie as she waited eight long, lonely years to meet her father? She had no choice but to endure—to persevere.

There is no doubt about it—"keeping heart" in difficult circumstances is not always easy. At times we think, wrongly, that God has forgotten us and is unaware of our needs. But consider the following verses:

> Why do you say, O Jacob, and complain, O Israel, "My way is hidden from the Lord; my cause is disregarded by my God"? Do you not know? Have you not heard? The Lord is the everlasting God, the Creator of the ends of the earth. He will not grow tired or weary, and his understanding no one can fathom. He gives strength to the weary and increases the power of the weak. Even youths grow tired and weary, and young men stumble and fall; but those who hope in the Lord will renew their strength. They will soar on wings like eagles; they will run and not grow weary, they will walk and not be faint. (Isaiah 40:27–31)

> But Zion said, "The Lord has forsaken me, the Lord has forgotten me." "Can a mother forget the baby at her breast and have no compassion on the child she has borne? Though she may forget, I will not forget you! See, I have engraved you on the palms of my hands . . . ." declares the Lord. (Isaiah 49:14-16)

List all the things that the above verses promise us.

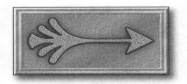 In order to persevere in hard times, we must choose to believe that our waiting will not only please the Lord, but also produce in us a strength of character that we might not otherwise develop.

Can you think of a time when having to wait for something that you wanted resulted in your growing spiritually? Explain.

Hebrews 12:2–3 says, "Let us fix our eyes on Jesus, the author and perfector of our faith, who *for the joy set before Him* endured the Cross, scorning its shame, and sat down at the right hand of the throne of God. Consider Him who endured such opposition from sinful men, so that you will not grow weary and *lose heart.*"

Is there anything that has caused you to grow weary and lose heart? If so, describe it here.

God's Word tells us in Nehemiah 8:10 that "the joy of the Lord is our strength." How can the joy of the Lord be your strength in the difficulties you face in your life right now?

The apostle Paul wrote: "We are hard pressed on every side, but not crushed; perplexed, but not in despair; persecuted, but not abandoned; struck down, but not destroyed. . . . *Therefore we do not lose heart . . . .* For our light and momentary troubles are achieving for us an eternal glory that far outweighs them all. So we fix our eyes not on what is seen, but on what is unseen. For what is seen is temporary, but what is unseen is eternal" (2 Corinthians 4:8–9, 16–18).

# A Joy to Others

All the girls had a grand reunion in the playroom, and Elsie was happy to see Harry Carrington, one of Lucy's older brothers, there too. The younger children, however, were not being cooperative. Little Flora Arnott was soon in tears, for Enna — so spoiled that it never occurred to her to be polite to a guest — had taken most of the building blocks that Flora was playing with.

Elsie tried to solve the dispute, but Enna flatly refused to share — and Elsie knew better than to start a quarrel with Enna, who was Mrs. Dinsmore's pampered pet. Then Elsie had an idea. She took Flora aside and said, "Pay no attention to Enna. I have something that you will really enjoy playing with. Will you wait right here while I get it?"

Sniffling a little, Flora nodded her head. Elsie ran from the playroom and was back in just a few moments. Cradled in her arm, she carried a beautiful baby doll dressed in delicate white lace and linen. Gently, she put the porcelain baby in Flora's arms and said, "This is my very best doll, Flora, and you must be very careful with it. My guardian gave it to me when I was even younger than you. He's dead now, so this doll means a great deal to me."

The little girl's blue eyes had widened with wonder. "Oh, Elsie," she said in almost a whisper, "I shall take very good care of it, I promise. It is so very pretty."

— *Elsie's Impossible Choice*, pages 27–28

From the previous lessons, we've learned that our joy is not based on circumstances or people; our joy comes from the Lord. In one sense, we cannot give joy to others; they, too, must find it in their love for Jesus. In another sense, though, as recipients of heavenly joy, we can spread what God has given us and make it easier for others to find joy in Him. This is perhaps one of the greatest gifts we can give to others.

List some of the ways that Elsie attempted to spread joy to those around her.

List several ways that you can bring joy to the members of your family and to other people in your life. Be specific.

We can do many practical deeds to bring joy to others: we can pray for them, we can assist them, we can cooperate with their work, we can befriend them, we can do kind things for them, we can encourage them in areas where they need it, and we can express gratitude for the things they do. Even a simple "thank you for your hard work" is a tremendous way to spread the Lord's joy to others.

 **In addition to what you can DO to bring joy to others, there are ways that you can BE a joy to others. You can *be* a joy to others by walking in and reflecting an attitude of thankfulness.**

No matter what our circumstances, we can always find something to be thankful for. And thankfulness releases joy! We see this in the life of Elsie. Even without a mother or father to love her, with the rejection of her stepmother and the constant harassment of her aunts and uncles, Elsie found things for which to be thankful. She was thankful for the love of Jesus; she was thankful to have the Word of God to sustain her; she was even thankful that she was healthy and not lame like her dear friend Herbert (see *Elsie's Endless Wait*, page 145).

List some things you are thankful for.

Now list some of the things you take for granted.

Think of a time that you forgot to thank someone who helped you or did something kind for you. Is it too late to thank them now?

Are you familiar with the story in Luke 17:12–19 of the ten lepers who came to Jesus? With their bodies covered with leprosy, they stood at a distance from Jesus and cried out, "Master, have pity on us!" Jesus told them, "Go, show yourselves to the priests," and, on their way, they were healed. Of these ten men, though, *just one* returned to give thanks to Jesus.

Which best describes the way you interact with Jesus and others? Are you like the nine men who did not return or like the one man who returned to thank Jesus? Explain.

The opposite of an attitude of thankfulness is an ungrateful, complaining, or grumbling attitude. God does not like complaining; neither do your parents, teachers or friends. *Complaining reflects a lack of gratitude.* Thankful people walk in joy, but ungrateful people find little joy.

Which kind of attitude do you think people most often see in you—gratitude or ingratitude—and why?

What changes, if any, can you make in your attitude or behavior to become more of a joy to others?

**Joy is a powerful instrument! One of the best ways we can share the love of God and the hope we have in Jesus is to display the fruit of joy in our own lives.**

# The Joy of Worship

That evening, Elsie and Horace shared what had become a very special time for Elsie — reading the Bible and singing hymns in the waning hours of the Sabbath. Elsie loved to sing with her father, her sweet voice blending with his deep bass. She talked with him about what she read in the Bible, asking him occasional questions which he was, even with all his learning and experience, scarcely capable of answering.

— *Elsie's Impossible Choice*, page 88

When we talked about joy earlier, we discussed how it exists even in sadness and does not depend on circumstances. Joy, rather, is a state of contentment that comes from resting in the promises of God. It could be said, then, that joy has many looks. Joy can appear happy and exuberant, but joy can also appear quiet, assured, and restful. The same stands true for worship. Worship can appear lively and excited, but it can also be quiet and gentle. As joy is a constant condition in the lives of those who love Jesus, worship, too, exists in everything that we do. That was true of Elsie's life. Because of her great love for the Lord, everything she did was a form of worship to the Lord! In other words, she lived a *lifestyle* of worship.

Look up the following verses in your Bible. Write each one out and then note the various expressions of worship that are described:

Ephesians 5:19–20 –

Psalm 9:1–2 –

Psalm 107:21–22 –

When we think about worshiping God, most of us think of singing songs. This is definitely worship, and quite pleasing to God! But worship involves even more than this.

When the Bible was written, it was originally written in the languages of Hebrew and Greek. The English word "worship" in those languages means "to bow down" or "to kneel."

 **When we worship God, we can physically bow and kneel, but we can also do these actions with our hearts. We can bow our hearts to Him.**

When we speak of worship, we think about praising God for who He is, and thanking Him for His love and faithfulness. We remember His power and His might. We want to tell Him how much we love Him, and we desire to show Him honor. From these things, you can see that worship is not just singing praises to the Lord. Worship can include any activity we perform if we are doing it to honor God or show that we adore Him. Acts of kindness can be a form of worship to God, and so can acts of obedience.

List some specific activities that you can do to worship God.

In 1 Peter 2:9 we're reminded that we are a chosen people, a royal priesthood, a holy nation, a people belonging to God. Why? The verse continues, *"That we may declare the praises of Him* who called us out of darkness into His wonderful light." Think about that for a moment. We were created to worship God. To enjoy God and declare His praises is our chief purpose in life.

Look back over this chapter. Ask the Holy Spirit to show you the most important things He wants you to remember. Put a star beside those truths and, in your own words, summarize below what He showed you.

Rewrite your thoughts as a prayer, asking God to help you grow and apply the truths He's taught you throughout the chapter.

Write out the memory verse for this chapter:

Write out Galatians 5:22–23, the memory verse for our entire study guide:

# CHAPTER

3

# Walking in Peace

# *Walking in Peace*

**by heart**

Do not be anxious about anything, but in everything, by prayer and petition, with thanksgiving, present your requests to God. And the peace of God, which transcends all understanding, will guard your hearts and your minds in Christ Jesus.

— PHILIPPIANS 4:6–7

## Peace With God

"Do you *really* love the Bible so? Will you tell me why," [Adelaide said to Rose].

"For its great and precious promises, Adelaide, and for its teachings about holy living. It offers inner peace and pardon from sin and eternal life," Rose said. "The Bible brings me the glad news of salvation offered as a free, unmerited gift. It tells me that Jesus died to save sinners such as me and that through Him, I am reconciled to God."

Adelaide could hear the deep emotion in her friend's voice as Rose went on, "I often find that my feelings and thoughts are not what they should be, and the blessed Bible tells me how my heart and mind can be renewed. When I find myself utterly unable to keep God's holy law, the Bible tells me of One who kept it for me and who willingly suffered for my sins," Rose said with a solemn passion that made her seem much older than her seventeen years.

Both women sat silently for a time. Then Adelaide's face clouded, and she said a little sternly, "You talk as if you were a great sinner, Rose, but I don't believe it. It's only your humility that makes you think like that. Why, what have you ever done? If you were a thief or a murderer or guilty of some terrible crime, I could understand your saying such things about yourself. Excuse me for this, Rose, but your language seems absurd for a refined, intelligent, and amiable young lady."

Gently, Rose responded to her friend's complaint. "'Man looks at the outward appearance, but God looks at the heart,'" she quoted. Then she explained, "From my earliest existence, God has required the undivided love of my whole heart, soul, strength, and mind; yet until the last two years, I was in rebellion against Him, not allowing Him to govern my life. For all my life, He has showered blessings on me. He has given me life and health, strength and friends — everything necessary for happiness. But I gave back nothing but ingratitude and rebellion. All that time I rejected His offers of pardon and reconciliation and resisted all the efforts of God's Holy Spirit to draw me to Him."

Rose's voice quivered, and her eyes brimmed with tears. "Can you not now see me as a sinner?"

Adelaide moved closer to her friend's side and put her arm around Rose's shoulders. "Don't think of these things, dear Rose," she gently admonished. "Religion is too gloomy for one as young as you."

"True religion is not gloomy at all," Rose answered, hugging Adelaide in return. "I never knew what true happiness was until I found Jesus. My sins often make me sad, but my faith in Him? Never."

— *Elsie's Endless Wait*, pages 20–21

Peace is something that most people would say they want more of in their lives—peace on the outside of them and, more importantly, peace on the inside.

How would you define peace?

In the above passage, Rose discussed with Adelaide the most important peace of all — *the inner peace that comes from being pardoned from sin and reconciled to God.* Rose was expressing to Adelaide the essence of feeling forgiven when she said, "I never knew what true happiness was until I found Jesus." We know that Elsie felt the same way, for she and Rose considered themselves "pilgrims on the same path" (see *Elsie's Endless Wait*, page 27). Even though Elsie suffered terrible hardships, she possessed peace in her relationship with Jesus Christ.

The Bible tells us that everyone has sinned and fallen short of the glory of God (Romans 3:23). As sinners, we cannot have a relationship with God because of His great holiness. But through the death of His Son, Jesus Christ, on our behalf, God provided a way for us to be restored in our relationship to Him (or reconciled). Once we accept Jesus into our hearts and are reconciled to God, we are at peace with our heavenly Father.

Have you been reconciled to God the Father through Jesus, His Son? If so, how did it happen? In other words, how did you come to Christ?

 **When you sin and disobey God, it disrupts the peace in your relationship with Him.**

How can you restore peace to your relationships withGod when you have sinned and disobeyed Him?

Through the apostle John, the Holy Spirit assures us, "My dear children, I write this to you so that you will not sin. But if anyone does sin, we have one who speaks to the Father in our defense — Jesus Christ, the Righteous One. He is the atoning sacrifice for our sins, and not only for ours but also for the sins of the whole world" (1 John 2:1–2). John continues to say, "If we confess our sins, he is faithful and just and will forgive us our sins and purify us from all unrighteousness" (1 John 1:9).

How does confessing our sins help restore our peace?

How can you restore peace to your relationships with your parents or teachers when you have disobeyed them?

Sometimes, we find ourselves stuck in a habit of sin. It seems no matter how we try, we keep falling into the same trap. If you feel stuck in a pattern of sin, you're not alone.

Even the apostle Paul got stuck. He said, "I do not understand what I do. For what I want to do I do not do, but what I hate I do . . . . I have the desire to do what is good, but I cannot carry it out. For what I do is not the good I want to do; no, the evil I do not want to do — this I keep on doing" (Romans 7:15–19).

Paul sounds pretty frustrated! Fortunately, Jesus has an unlimited supply of forgiveness. Never think that you can't go to Him once more with the same confession and try again with His help to overcome a fault. Jesus is the One you should turn to for help to break the habit of sin. In Hebrews 4:15, we're told, "For we do not have a high priest who is unable to sympathize with our weaknesses, but we have one who has been tempted in every way, just as we are — yet was without sin." The passage continues, *"Let us approach the throne of grace with confidence, so that we may receive mercy and find grace to help us in our time of need"* (v. 16).

What do those verses say to you?

What habits of sin do you have that you would like to see broken? List them here and then take some time to pray and ask the Lord and His Holy Spirit to help you conquer them.

## Care-free

When Rose Allison had left the schoolroom, Elsie got up from her desk and knelt down with her Bible before her. In her own simple words, she poured out her story to the dear Savior she loved so well, confessing that when she had done right and suffered for it, she had not endured the injustice. Earnestly, she prayed to be made like the meek and lowly Jesus, and as she prayed, her tears fell on the pages of her Bible. But when she stood again, Elsie's load of sorrow was gone, and as always, her heart was light with a sweet sense of peace and pardon.

—*Elsie's Endless Wait*, page 25

The prior scene takes place after Miss Rose had found Elsie sobbing in the schoolroom and sought to comfort her. Elsie had been treated unkindly by Arthur and unfairly by her teacher. Talking with Miss Rose did indeed comfort Elsie, but it was afterwards, when Elsie knelt down with her Bible and talked with the Lord, that she found real peace and release from her burden. Elsie's cares and despair were dissolved at the altar of God's grace!

At times, you have, no doubt, experienced feelings of frustration, sorrow, fear, guilt, confusion, discouragement, anxiety, anger, or despair. Perhaps a friend betrayed you. Maybe you weren't doing well in school, or you felt angry or upset with yourself or someone else for some reason. Maybe your family was struggling financially, or you and your siblings were arguing a lot. One minute, you felt okay and thought everything was fine, but the next minute, you found yourself upset and unable to get your insides to calm down again. This happens to all of us.

What are some of the things that normally cause you to worry, be upset, restless or angry?

How do you react when these things take place?

Here is a list of things people sometimes do when they are worried, upset, restless or angry. Mark an "x" in the boxes that apply to you.

❏ drastic shifts in mood

❏ want to be alone

❏ mean or rude to others

❏ outbursts of anger

❏ nightmares or bad dreams

❏ trying too hard to achieve things

❏ depression or self-pity

❏ can't sleep or sleep too much

❏ being afraid of different things all the time

❏ overly concerned with appearance

❏ other: _____

Sometimes, we're the last ones to see these behaviors in ourselves, but it is often the case that our actions speak louder than our words. Whether we see them or not, these behaviors are evidence of a lack of peace.

Consider the following passages of Scripture:

When the prophet Isaiah foretold the coming Messiah, he wrote, "For to us a child is born, to us a Son is given, and the government will be on his shoulders. And he will be called Wonderful Counselor, Mighty God, Everlasting Father, *Prince of Peace*. Of the increase of his government *and peace* there will be no end" (Isaiah 9:6–7).

Several hundred years later, shortly after Jesus ascended from the grave, He returned to His disciples. Standing among them, He said, "'*Peace be with you!*' . . . . Again Jesus said, '*Peace be with you!* As the Father has sent me, I am sending you.' And with that he breathed on them and said, '*Receive the Holy Spirit*'" (John 20:19–22).

Wow! Can you imagine? If you have received Jesus, the Holy Spirit of God lives in you! What promise! What hope! Is there anything you can't overcome? After all, "The one who is in you is greater than the one who is in the world" (1 John 4:4). The Prince of Peace sits enthroned in your heart! Ephesians 2:14 tells us, "For *he himself* is our peace . . ." *As Elsie discovered, Jesus is the answer for every burden and every stress!* Isaiah 26:3 promises, "You will keep in perfect peace him whose mind is steadfast, because he trusts in you."

Look again at our memory verse, Philippians 4:6–7. "Do not be anxious *about anything*, but *in everything*, by prayer and petition, with thanksgiving, present your requests to God. And the peace of God, which transcends all understanding, will guard your hearts and your minds in Christ Jesus."

Anything? Everything? Those are pretty big words! But because the Holy Spirit of God lives within us, we can become free from the cares of this world — *every single one of them.* Does that mean that the things we are concerned about disappear? No, but if we ask, the Holy Spirit can set our hearts and minds at peace about those things. He can replace your worry and anxiety with peace. And not just any peace, but a peace that passes all understanding. That is God's promise to you!

 **If we will learn to do what Philippians 4:6–7 tells us to do, we can be "care-free!"**

Take some time right now to lift your cares and worries up to the Lord in prayer. "By prayer and petition, with thanksgiving, present your requests to God." Ask Him to replace your worries with the peace of the Holy Spirit.

# In the Face of Fear

*L*ora still looked a little pale, and more thoughtful than Elsie could remember. Lora didn't say anything at first, then suddenly she burst out, "Oh, Elsie! I can't help thinking, what if we'd all been killed? Where would we all be now? Where would I be? I believe you would have gone straight to heaven, but I? I would be like the rich man the minister talked about this morning, lifting up my eyes in torment."

Lora covered her eyes and a shudder ran through her. Then she said, "We were all so afraid, but you, Elsie. What kept you from being afraid?"

"I was thinking of a Bible verse I know. 'Even though I walk through the valley of the shadow of death, I will fear no evil, for you are with me.' God said for us not to be afraid because He is with us. I knew that Jesus was there with me, and if I were killed, I'd wake up again in His arms. That's why I wasn't so afraid."

—*Elsie's Endless Wait*, pages 127–128

*F*ear is a powerful force. If we imagine an intruder breaking into our homes, or humiliating ourselves in front of the entire class, or other types of fearful experiences, we tremble and shrink back. A part of fear's force is that it often strikes us completely unaware. Like a sneaky villain, it silently seeps into our hearts.

List the fears you struggle with.

Rest assured, the fears you have listed are shared by many others your age. Fear is a very real problem facing young people today. You might think, however, that young people are the only ones who struggle with fears of various sorts. But if you talk with adults, you will find that they have fears too. However, because adults have lived longer, they have learned how to deal with their fears.

**Adults, such as your parents, teachers, and youth leaders, can be a valuable source of wisdom and encouragement for you in dealing with your fears.**

There is good news for those who want to conquer fear. The Bible teaches us that God has an antidote for fear — a peace that transcends (or passes) all understanding. Remember the promise of our memory verse? Write out Philippians 4:6–7 here.

Jesus said to His disciples, "Peace I leave with you; my peace I give you. I do not give to you as the world gives. Do not let your hearts be troubled and do not be afraid" (John 14:27). He spoke these words to His disciples as He told them He would be going to the Father. At that time, they did not truly understand what was about to happen; but Jesus knew. He understood that they would feel hopeless and afraid. Jesus knew there would be cause for fear, yet he assured them, "*My* peace I give to you."

In the previous excerpt, Elsie explained to Lora why she was not afraid for their lives when the horses bolted and their carriage careened out of control down the road. Elsie was not afraid because she fully trusted in the love of God.

Think about God's awesome love, strength, and power for a minute. Focus on His unchanging, tender love for you. His Word says:

"The name of the Lord is a strong tower; the righteous run to it and are safe" (Proverbs 18:10).

"If you make the Most High your dwelling—even the Lord, who is my refuge—then no harm will befall you, no disaster will come near your tent. For he will command his angels concerning you to guard you in all your ways" (Psalm 91:9–11).

Describe a time you were afraid and felt alone. How did you respond to your fear?

 **When we are afraid, we must choose to believe God's Word instead of our emotions.**

Can you recall a time where Jesus gave you peace in a situation where you were afraid? What happened?

Elsie Dinsmore *believed* the promises that she found in the Word of God. "Great peace have they who love your law, and nothing can make them stumble," says Psalm 119:165. The promises in God's Word built her hope and strengthened her faith in God. That is why knowing the Word was so important to Elsie. In times of fear, she would remind herself of God's promises and His faithfulness.

Jesus says to us, "Even the very hairs of your head are all numbered. So don't be afraid; you are worth more than many sparrows" (Matthew 10:30–31). In the face of fearful circumstances, we can—and must—trust God.

# Trusting in Discipline

"I've been so bad today, Aunt Chloe. I'm afraid I'll never be as good as Papa wants me to be. I know he's disappointed with me because I disobeyed him today," Elsie said, as her tears rolled down her cheeks.

"Then you must go to the throne of grace and tell the Lord Jesus about your troubles," Chloe said. "Remember what the Bible tells us: 'If anybody does sin, we have one who speaks to the Father in our defense — Jesus Christ the Righteous One.' Speak to Jesus, darling, and ask Him to help you trust your Papa and obey him even when you don't understand his reasons."

"You're right, Aunt Chloe. Jesus will forgive me and give me right thoughts and feelings," Elsie proclaimed. Then she wrapped her arms around her nursemaid's neck for a loving embrace.

She told Chloe of her father's directions and began to prepare for bed. She had stopped crying, but her face was still sad and troubled. When she was in her nightdress, with her hair brushed and tucked in her nightcap, Elsie took her little Bible and in a trembling voice, read from the twelfth chapter of Proverbs: "Whoever loves discipline loves knowledge, but he who hates correction is stupid."

"I must learn to be grateful for Papa's correction," she told herself, "but Jesus will have to help me." Sighing, she knelt by her bed and prayed. Chloe, watching her little girl, was filled with compassion, and she gave the child every assurance of her own love before tucking her into bed.

—*Elsie's Endless Wait*, pages 93–94

$\mathcal{B}$ecause we associate the word "discipline" with punishment, we struggle to believe that our loving, merciful Father God would discipline us. After all, didn't Jesus die for our sins? Why, then, would God need to punish us? Before we advance any further in this study, perhaps we should come to a fuller understanding of what it actually means to be disciplined.

There is a word in the Bible that comes from the word "discipline." Can you think of it? (Hint: there were twelve of them!)

The word we are talking about is "disciple." To be a disciple means you have been specially selected as a pupil. It is both an honor and a privilege.

The twelve men that walked with Jesus aren't the only ones called as *disciples*. Jesus put out the word to all who would follow Him, saying, "Therefore go and make *disciples* of all nations" (Matthew 28:19). As He continues to disciple us, Jesus invites us to join Him in His ongoing work of discipling others.

If we define a disciple as a student or a trainee, discipline, then, could be considered instruction, mentoring, or training. When someone mentors or trains us, he or she invests in our lives. It is a privilege to be discipled by someone more mature in the Lord who can help us grow in our faith.

How, other than by your parents' discipline, have you been discipled? List at least three people in different roles (friend, coach, teacher, etc.) and explain how these people have invested themselves to bring out your best.

The Lord promises to discipline us, for Hebrews 12:6 says, ". . . the Lord disciplines those He loves." He is committed to us in a manner far superior to even the best, most loving earthly parents.

We read on page 198 of *Elsie's Endless Wait* that Horace's desire was to protect Elsie from all dangers and to "save her from the unhappiness of so many children who were raised without discipline," like his own brother Arthur, who was a liar and a sneak. Horace did not want such a fate to befall his beloved child.

Most readers find some of Mr. Dinsmore's practices unusually severe. As *Elsie's Impossible Choice* comes to a close, Horace himself begins to see his manner as overly harsh. We must recognize, though, that all the while Elsie endured his harsh discipline—for example, when she had to sit motionless on the piano bench in the afternoon heat or spend months isolated from the two people she loved the most—Elsie's heavenly Father hovered over her like a loving, ever-attentive parent. Not for one moment was Elsie without a perfect Abba Father, a gentle and merciful "Dad" who stood watching, loving, and yes, disciplining.

In the harsh discipline of her father, how did Elsie keep her mind steadfast? Include in your answer things Elsie *did* do, as well as things Elsie *did not* do.

How should you respond to the discipline of those in authority over you, whether you feel they are right or wrong?

In the passage above from pages 93–94 of *Elsie's Endless Wait*, Elsie read from the twelfth chapter of Proverbs: "Whoever loves discipline loves knowledge, but he who hates correction is stupid." "I must learn to be grateful for Papa's correction," she told herself, "but Jesus will have to help me."

On another occasion in *Elsie's Endless Wait*, we read the following:

With [her father's] forgiveness, [Elsie] went to her punishment. But once again, she found comfort in the pages of her worn Bible. She searched for some time before finding the verse she wanted in the twelfth chapter of Hebrews: "No discipline seems pleasant at the time, but painful. Later on, however, it produces a harvest of righteousness and peace for those who have been trained by it." Elsie recited the verse over and over to herself until she felt her hope renewed.

—*Elsie's Endless Wait*, page 82

**Elsie believed in the promise that the discipline she was undergoing would produce "a harvest of righteousness and peace" for her if she allowed herself to be trained by it.**

Rather than become anxious and angry about things, Elsie allowed the peace of God to guard her heart and mind in Christ Jesus.

Can you recite our memory verse, Philippians 4:6–7, yet?

# Makers of Peace

Elsie went back to her work with renewed diligence and faithfully completed all her assignments. When Miss Day returned from the fair, Elsie was able to recite her geography lesson without a single mistake. Her arithmetic problems were solved correctly, and the writing in her copybook was neat and careful.

But Miss Day, who had been in an ill-tempered mood all day, now seemed angry that Elsie did not give her another excuse for criticism. The governess handed the copybook back to the child and remarked sarcastically, "I see that you can do your duties well enough when you choose."

The injustice of Miss Day's words struck Elsie, and she wanted to protest that she had tried just as hard that morning. But she remembered her earlier, rash words and what they had cost her. Instead of defending herself, she meekly said, "I'm sorry I didn't do better this morning, though I really did try. I'm still more sorry for the disrespectful remark I made, and I ask your pardon."

"You ought to be sorry," replied Miss Day sharply, "and I hope you really are. You were very impertinent, and you deserved a more severe punishment than you received. Now go, and never let me hear anything like that from you again."

Elsie's eyes filled with tears again, but remembering how Jesus made no reply in the face of his accusers, she said nothing to Miss Day's hateful remarks. She simply put away her books and slate and left the schoolroom.

—*Elsie's Endless Wait*, pages 25–26

Are you familiar with the portion of Scripture that we call the Beatitudes, from the Sermon on the Mount? Found in Matthew, chapter 5, the Beatitudes list several promises that begin with "Blessed are . . . ." Among these promises, we read: "Blessed are the peacemakers, for they will be called sons of God" (v. 9).

Do you think of yourself as a peacemaker? Why or why not?

Do you think your family and friends see you as a peacemaker? Why or why not?

So how do we live as peacemakers? Here are some peacemaking principles that will help you.

### A PEACEMAKER LOOKS THROUGH GOD'S EYES RATHER THAN HER OWN.

Scripture tells us that "man looks at the outward appearance, but the Lord looks at the heart" (Isaiah 16:7). Our heavenly Father not only sees us through the righteousness of His Son, but He sees us through the resurrection of Jesus as well. This means that God sees us as we will one day be when perfected from every sin. Rather than condemning us or criticizing us, our Father treats us as if we've already attained this glorious image!

Paul encourages us to look at others the same way. He says, "So from now on we regard no one from a worldly point of view" (2 Corinthians 5:16). *Because the Holy Spirit dwells inside us, we can (and should) see others as God sees us—precious in His sight.* God wants us to be committed to other people and persistent in our efforts to bring about peace whenever there are problems in a relationship. Peacemakers trust in God's magnificent power to overcome difficulties.

### A PEACEMAKER "SETTLES MATTERS QUICKLY WITH HER ADVERSARIES" (MATTHEW 5:25).

Elsie asked her father, "Will you forgive me, Papa? I won't be able to sleep if you're still angry with me" (*Elsie's Endless Wait*, page 82). Peacemakers love peace! They "do not let the sun go down while [they] are still angry" (see Ephesians 4:26). They won't hold grudges, give the silent treatment, or allow others to sit in the hurt that they've caused. Peacemakers move toward forgiveness and resolution immediately.

Jesus said, "Therefore, if you are offering your gift at the altar and there remember that your brother has something against you, leave your gift there in front of the altar. First go and be reconciled to your brother . . ." (Matthew 5:23–24).

To bring a gift to the altar means to come before the Lord to give Him love, honor and praise. In this verse, God is saying you must be a peacemaker before He can accept these gifts. If you have an unresolved issue with another person, you must go to them and ask for forgiveness if you have hurt them or forgive them if they have hurt you. Work it out together. Resolve the issue and bring peace back into your relationship. If we want to receive the fullness of God's forgiveness, we must be willing to seek out the forgiveness of those whom we have hurt.

 **A PEACEMAKER PUTS OTHERS IN A GOOD LIGHT.**

A peacemaker refrains from speaking ill of others. A peacemaker chooses, instead, to say only that which is life-giving and positive. Like a valued photograph, a peacemaker positions friends *and foes* in the best possible light so that others will see their best.

What do you typically do when someone comes to you and starts gossiping or speaking negatively about someone else? Be honest in your answer.

How would you feel if you knew that others were gossiping about you?

The Bible tells us that "love covers a multitude of sins" (1 Peter 4:8). When we walk in love, we don't expose the faults and flaws of others. Simply put, peacemakers refuse to gossip. Even when wronged, peacemakers decline from talking about the wrongs committed by others. James 3:18 promises, "Peacemakers who sow in peace will raise a harvest of righteousness."

**When we have broken relationships with others, it not only creates a gap in those relationships, but with Jesus as well. However, reconciliation of relationships opens the gates of our hearts to the Holy Spirit and restores the peace.**

Pause and examine your life for a few moments. Ask the Holy Spirit to show you relationships you now have which are broken and need to be repaired. Ask Him to help you recall every person whom you hold something against, as well as those who have reason to be angry with you. Make a note of these names in the two lists that follow. Pray and ask

the Lord to show you what He would like you do to be a peacemaker and restore the peace of His Holy Spirit in those relationships.

| PERSON | THEIR OFFENSE AGAINST ME | HOW TO RESTORE PEACE |
|---|---|---|
|  |  |  |

| PERSON | MY OFFENSE AGAINST THEM | HOW TO RESTORE PEACE |
|---|---|---|
|  |  |  |

Look back over this chapter. Ask the Holy Spirit to show you the most important things He wants you to remember. Put a star beside those truths and, in your own words, summarize below what He showed you.

Rewrite your thoughts as a prayer, asking God to help you grow and apply the truths He's taught you throughout the chapter.

Write out the memory verse for this chapter:

Write out Galatians 5:22–23, the memory verse for our entire study guide:

CHAPTER

# *Walking in Patience*

## Lesson 1
*More Than Tolerance*

## Lesson 2
*Waiting on God*

## Lesson 3
*Severe Patience*

## Lesson 4
*Patient When Misunderstood*

## Lesson 5
*Patient With Ourselves*

# *Walking in Patience*

*A*s a prisoner for the Lord, then, I urge you to live a life worthy of the calling you have received. Be completely humble and gentle; be patient, bearing with one another in love.
— EPHESIANS 4:1–2

## More Than Tolerance

*E*lsie had been knitting, and suddenly she held up the purse. "See!" she exclaimed. "It's all done except for putting on the tassel. Isn't it pretty, Aunt Chloe? Do you think Miss Allison will be pleased?"

It was, Chloe agreed, a very pretty purse, beautifully knit in crimson and gold, and she was sure Miss Allison would be delighted. They were admiring the purse when Enna opened the door and came in. Although Elsie tried to conceal the purse in her pocket, it was too late. Enna had seen it, and she ran to Elsie, crying, "Just give that to me, Elsie!"

When Elsie refused, explaining that it was a gift for Miss Allison, Enna raised her voice even more and demanded, "Give it to me now, or I'll go and tell Mamma!"

"I'll let you hold it for a few moments, if you promise not to soil it," Elsie said gently. "And if you like, I'll get more silk and beads and make you a purse just like it. But I can't give it to you because then I wouldn't have time to make another one for Miss Allison."

But Enna was adamant: "I want that now, and I want it to keep!" She tried to snatch the purse from Elsie's hand, but Elsie held it up out of the screaming child's reach. Finally Enna gave up and ran crying from the room.

Chloe locked the door, remarking that it was a pity they had forgotten to lock it earlier. "I'm afraid Miss Enna will get her mother to make you give it up," she said sadly.

Elsie went back to her work, but her eyes were full of tears and her hands trembled with agitation.

Chloe's fears were well founded, of course, and it was not very long before they heard hasty steps in the hallway and the rattling of the doorknob. When the door refused to open, Mrs. Dinsmore's booming voice commanded, "Open this door immediately!"

Chloe looked at Elsie. Tearfully, the little girl slipped the purse into her pocket again and lifted her heart in a quick prayer for patience and meekness, for she knew she would need both.

Chloe slowly unlocked the door, and Mrs. Dinsmore entered, with a sobbing Enna hanging onto her hand. The woman's face was flushed a bright red, and she spoke angrily to Elsie. "What is the meaning of this, you little good-for-nothing? Why are you always tormenting my poor Enna? Where is the pitiful thing that this fuss is all about? Let me see it at once!"

Elsie took the purse from her pocket. Her voice trembled as she said, "It's the purse I was making for Miss Allison. I'll make one just like it for Enna, but I cannot give her this one."

"You *can* not? You *will* not is what you mean. But I say you *shall*, and I am mistress in this house. Give it to Enna this instant. I will not have her crying her eyes out just to humor you in your whims."

— *Elsie's Endless Wait*, pages 39–40

When we think of patience, we normally think of having to wait. In that context, learning to walk in patience involves learning to endure delays without complaint. But before we think more about that aspect of patience, let's discuss another kind of patience. Webster's College Dictionary describes it as "the bearing of provocation, annoyance, misfortune or pain without complaint, loss of temper, or anger." The above encounter between Elsie and Enna is a perfect example!

Describe how you would have responded to Enna if you had been in Elsie's situation?

Now describe what you think Elsie's inner thoughts and feelings were during and after her encounter with Enna.

Elsie had every reason to resist Enna's selfish and unfair demands for the purse she had made for Miss Allison. Elsie's patience was tested to its very limits. Yet she responded with what appears to us to be unbelievable graciousness and superhuman patience. Elsie even offered to purchase new materials to make one exactly like it for Enna! How did Elsie do it? She relied on the power of the Holy Spirit of God! Without the love of God and the power of the Holy Spirit in her heart, she would not have had the *desire* to be patient with Enna, let alone the *ability* to do it.

Think about Galatians 5:22–23, our memory verse for this whole study guide, in relation to the above excerpt. In the space below, write down which of the nine dimensions of the fruit of the Spirit you think Elsie demonstrated in her response to Enna. Then next to each one you list, write down how she demonstrated it.

<u>**Fruit of the Spirit**</u>        <u>**How Demonstrated**</u>

There are many times when, without the help of God's Holy Spirit, patience seems to be humanly impossible! Whether it's pesky younger brothers or sisters, mean older siblings, frustrations in the classroom, or other annoyances, our patience is put to the test regularly. List three incidents in your life during the past week that tried your patience and how you responded.

Patience is far more than just putting up with someone or something that annoys you. It is an outward act of composure and an inward state of heart.

**Patience means more than just tolerating others; it involves a decision of the heart to put other's needs above your own and to wait to have your needs met.**

As we study the fruit of the Holy Spirit, particularly this gift of patience, we see that far more than self-discipline and a desire to obey God are involved. Discipline and obedience can produce resentment, drudgery, and eventually, failure, unless they are motivated by a genuine love for God. Genuine love for God will lead one to obey God's commandments because of "want to," not "have to." Love for God *inspires* obedience!

In Ephesians 4:1–2, our memory verse for this chapter, Paul says to us, "As a prisoner for the Lord, then, I urge you to live a life worthy of the calling you have received. Be completely humble and gentle; *be patient, bearing with one another in love*." Only through the power of God's Holy Spirit within us can we bear with others in love.

# Waiting on God

Elsie clapped her hands together and dropped down onto the sofa. The letter from Rose, so highly prized a few moments before, drifted unnoticed to the floor. The child's thoughts were now far away, imagining the father she didn't know as he crossed the ocean for home. She tried to picture how he would look, how he would speak, and how he would feel about her.

"Oh, will he love me?" she asked herself aloud. "Will he let me love him? Will he take me in his arms and call me his own darling child?"

But there was no one to answer her anxious questions. She would just have to wait and let the slow wheel of time turn until her father's longed-for, and somehow frightful, arrival.

—*Elsie's Endless Wait*, page 50

Has someone ever said to you, "Be patient?" If you're like most of us, you've probably heard that several times in your life (and not been too happy to hear it). Think back to an incident when someone said that to you. Why were these words spoken? What did the person who said those words want you to do?

In the passage from *Elsie's Endless Wait* above, sadly, the object of Elsie's anticipation wasn't a toy . . . or a birthday . . . or graduation . . . or even a friend. A child virtually alone in the world, Elsie yearned for the arms of a parent to hold her. And Elsie waited. And waited. And waited. She had no choice but to "wait and let the slow wheel of time turn until her father's longed-for, and somehow frightful, arrival." After waiting from month to month, then year to year, for eight long years, her heart was weary with its almost hopeless waiting. *Even though Elsie had a strong faith in God, that does not mean that it was easy for her to be patient.*

In addition to the previous definition, Webster's College Dictionary also defines patience as "an ability or willingness to suppress restlessness or annoyance when confronted with delay" or a "quiet, steady perseverance."

List some things in your life that you're waiting for: perhaps a future event . . . something you've been saving for . . . working towards . . . praying about . . . etc.

People and circumstances, undoubtedly, are involved in your wait; otherwise you would already have what you want. Regardless of these factors, ultimately it is God that we actually wait upon.

**Because our Lord rules sovereignly over the entire universe, when it comes to the longings of our heart, we wait not for people or events, but for God Himself to respond. With just a word from His lips, He can provide for our every need. Sometimes, though, our heavenly Father says, "Wait."**

Write down some of the reasons that God might have you waiting for the things you listed above.

During our difficult times of waiting, we can take comfort in the fact that God understands just what we are feeling. Consider His unending patience with us. Think about how much He longs for everyone to come to know Him and how long He is having to wait. We are not alone in our waiting.

## Severe Patience

But Elsie still lingered, hoping for some token of his forgiveness. Sensing what she wanted, Horace considered what to do. With a hint of impatience, he said at last, "No, Elsie, I will not kiss you good night. You have been entirely too naughty. Now go straight to your room at once."

Could she *ever* win her father's love? The wait seemed endless at times. In her bed that night, Elsie searched her little Bible for words of hope. And she found them in the promise of God's eternal love: "For I am convinced that neither death nor life, neither angels nor demons, neither the present nor the future, nor any powers, neither height nor depth, nor anything else in all creation, will be able to separate us from the love of God that is in Christ Jesus our Lord." Whatever else happened to her, God's love would be with her always.

—*Elsie's Endless Wait*, page 138

The above scene takes place after Elsie's father finally came home. Unfortunately for Elsie, however, her waiting did not end upon his return. After eight years of waiting to meet him, Elsie had to continue to wait for her father to begin to love her. She had to *persevere* in her patience.

As we learned in chapter two, to persevere means to continue or persist at something despite obstacles, opposition, or difficulties. Remember our memory verse from that chapter, James 1:2–4? Write it out in the space below.

Jesus loves perseverance! He commends the saints often for persevering in their work and in their faith.

**So important is our ability to persevere that Jesus goes out of His way to develop that strength in our lives. In fact, Jesus may sometimes arrange our circumstances to include extended periods of waiting, enduring trials, and the testing of our faith, in order to produce this precious perseverance in us.**

Perseverance is like the little pink bunny in the TV commercial that keeps going and going and going, or the pony express rider of days past, who carried the mail through sleet and snow, floods, and threat of Indian attack. Perseverance keeps going, despite difficulties or challenges. Perseverance *refuses* to quit.

Romans 5:3 tells us that suffering produces perseverance. Like muscles, perseverance grows stronger as demands are placed on it. Through our trials and our enduring of them, we become stronger and stronger until we are eventually, with God's help, able to bear things we never imagined.

When Rose Allison heard about Elsie's lonely birth, the death of her mother and separation from her father, as well as her sad position among the Dinsmores, she understood Elsie's unusual maturity. Miss Allison had never before known someone so young who was so strong in faith. *But Elsie did not start out strong; she had been persevering over time and little by little she grew in her faith.*

Think back to a difficult season in your life. Can you now see proof of godly character that wasn't there *prior* to your struggles? Explain what happened here.

You see, the Holy Spirit is actually making each of us into heroes! Really. God's Spirit is conforming us into the image of the Ultimate Hero: Jesus. Think of the great perseverance of Jesus—He endured the Cross.

We're told in Hebrews 12:1 to "run with *perseverance* the race marked out for us." What do you think is the "race marked out" for you?

Now list the obstacles and challenges that require perseverance in order for you to cross "the finish line" in your race.

Pause and take a moment to ask the Holy Spirit to bring to mind anything you may have given up on too soon. As you write it below, ask the Lord to restore your ability to persevere.

None of us comes equipped with the full measure of perseverance. As we yield to the God-ordained circumstances in our lives, God strengthens and develops the fruit of His Spirit into what we might call "*severe* patience"—patience taken to the extreme. Severe patience allows us to bear all things through the power of the Holy Spirit—even the extreme annoyances of people like Enna!

# Patient When Misunderstood

*E*lsie remained in the middle of the room; she didn't dare to approach him, however much she wanted to. While she stood there, not knowing what to do, the door swung open, and Enna, looking rosy and happy, ran in and rushed to her brother. She climbed on his knee, put her chubby arms around his neck, and pleaded for a kiss.

"You shall have it, little pet," Horace laughed. Tossing down his paper, he hugged Enna warmly. "*You* are not afraid of me, are you?" he asked playfully, and added pointedly, "or sorry that I have come home?"

"No, indeed," Enna said.

Horace glanced at Elsie to see her reaction. Her eyes had filled with tears, and she could not stop herself thinking that Enna had taken her place and was receiving the love that should be hers. Horace read her reaction correctly, although he misunderstood its source. "She's jealous," he thought. "I cannot tolerate jealous people." He gave her a look that clearly displayed his displeasure, and Elsie, cut to the quick, had to leave the room to hide her tears.

—*Elsie's Endless Wait*, page 56

Do you usually feel the need to defend and protect yourself when you're misunderstood? What causes you to want to explain and tell your side?

In case you find it difficult to identify with the above questions, imagine yourself in this scenario: You and one of your closest friends have a serious argument. Afterwards, she tells your circle of friends that you said and did things that you didn't. Now, many of your friends are talking about you, and some aren't speaking to you. How would you respond, and why? (Be honest.)

In the above situation, most of us would be very quick to jump to our own defense. But the Bible shows us a different way to handle it—being patient and entrusting our defense to God. It says of Jesus that, "He committed no sin, and no deceit was found in his mouth. When they hurled their insults at him, he did not retaliate; when he suffered, he made no threats. Instead, *he entrusted himself to him who judges justly*" (1 Peter 2:22–23).

When it says that Jesus entrusted himself "to him who judges justly," it was referring to our Heavenly Father. Jesus did not stand up for Himself in the face of His accusers because He trusted God the Father and knew that the only opinion of Him that mattered was His Father's opinion and that God could, and would, reveal the truth about Jesus in His perfect timing.

How can that attitude of Jesus help us when we are misunderstood by others?

As we know, Elsie was often misunderstood and treated unfairly because of people's mistaken ideas about her. In the passage above, Elsie's father wrongly believed that Elsie was sorry that he had come home. Not true! Elsie had waited eight long and incredibly lonely years to see her father—she had dreamed of him day and night. Horace's belief could not have been further from the truth!

Yet, rather than defend herself, Elsie entrusted her fate (and her father's opinions about her) to the God who loved her. And she waited on Him to defend her. What an amazing perspective!

 **Because Elsie knew God's love, she was able to be patient even when it hurt—and even when she was terribly misunderstood. Patience enabled her to *wait in God's care*.**

Patience, remember, is the ability to wait to have our own needs met. It enables us to yield to the circumstances before us. When we rest in the promises of God, we can be patient in any situation.

# Patient With Ourselves

> ith a fresh burst of tears, she sobbed out her misery. "I — I didn't do it! I didn't bear it patiently. They weren't fair, and I was punished when I wasn't to blame. Then I — I got angry. I'm afraid that I'll never be like Jesus. Never!"
>
> …. Rose wrapped her arm around the child's waist. "My poor Elsie," she said. "That is your name, isn't it?"
>
> "Yes, ma'am. Elsie Dinsmore."
>
> "Well, Elsie, as you probably know, becoming like Jesus is the work of a lifetime, and we all stumble along the way. But Jesus understands, dear."
>
> "Yes ma'am," Elsie said. "I know He does, but I'm so sorry that I've grieved Him and displeased Him. I do love Him, and I want so much to be like Him."
>
> Rose stroked Elsie's hair and spoke tenderly, "But remember Elsie, God's love for us is *far* greater than we could ever imagine and it doesn't depend on our goodness, because none of us can be good enough on our own. It is Jesus' righteousness that is credited to our account. You must have patience, little one. His Holy Spirit in you will bring about the purity of heart you desire."
>
> —*Elsie's Endless Wait*, pages 13–14

When Elsie sobbed, through a burst of tears, "I'm afraid that I'll never be like Jesus. Never!" her frustration and disappointment sounds like that of the apostle Paul when he said, "I have the desire to do what is good, but I cannot carry it out" (Romans 7:18).

Have you ever felt disappointed in yourself? Have you ever asked yourself, "What's wrong with me? Why can't I do better?" All the while, though, deep inside of you, you know that you can do better — that's what's so frustrating. Describe a time when you've wrestled with emotions like these.

What type of circumstances cause you to feel this way (for example, criticism from others, feeling like you embarrassed yourself, comparing yourself with people, making a mistake, etc.)?

With Jesus as her first love, and her heart's desire to please Him, sometimes Elsie forgot to be patient with herself. Miss Allison lovingly reminded her, "Becoming like Jesus is the work of a lifetime, and we all stumble along the way." She also read Elsie Hebrews 4:15, which tells us that Jesus understands our weaknesses and offers us mercy and grace to help us in our time of need.

**If you feel like you fall short, you're not alone. The truth is that every one of us falls short often. But God calls us to be patient with *everyone* (1 Thessalonians 5:14). That includes ourselves!**

What do you think it means for you to be patient with yourself?

Take a moment now to seek God's grace and mercy and ask Him for help in the areas where you feel you are weak.

The fruit of patience frees us from our fears and concerns about our shortcomings, past mistakes, and inabilities. Knowing we are loved and that God is patient with us, we are able to be patient and to extend mercy . . . even to ourselves. In our waiting to become more like Jesus, we can be confident in the promise of Philippians 1:6—that He who began a good work in us will carry it on to completion!

Look back over this chapter. Ask the Holy Spirit to show you the most important things He wants you to remember. Put a star beside those truths and, in your own words, summarize below what He showed you.

Rewrite your thoughts as a prayer, asking God to help you grow and apply the truths He's taught you throughout the chapter.

Write out the memory verse for this chapter:

Write out Galatians 5:22–23, the memory verse for our entire study guide:

# CHAPTER

**5**

# *Walking in Kindness*

# Walking in Kindness

**by heart**

Be kind and compassionate to one another, forgiving each other, just as in Christ God forgave you.

— EPHESIANS 4:32

## Behind the Scenes With Kindness

"Elsie is the only person who can help you," Lora was saying. "She has plenty of money, and you know that she is generous. But if I were you, I'd be ashamed to ask her, after the way you treated her yesterday."

"I wish I hadn't teased her," Arthur agreed, "but it's so much fun that I can't help myself."

"Well, I know that I wouldn't ask a favor of anybody whom I had treated so meanly," Lora said finally, and Elsie heard footsteps as the older girl walked away.

Elsie worked at her drawing, but her thoughts were of Arthur. What was it that he wanted? Was this an opportunity for her to return good for evil? . . . Without thinking, Elsie went to him, laid her hand on his shoulder, and asked if there was anything she could do to help.

"No — yes — " he answered haltingly. "I don't like to ask after — after —"

"Oh, never mind yesterday," Elsie said quickly. "I don't care about that now. I went to the fair today, and it was even better because I went with Aunt Adelaide and Miss Allison. So tell me what you want."

Encouraged, Arthur explained, "I saw a beautiful model of a ship when we were in the city yesterday, and I've set my heart on having it. It only costs five dollars, but my pocket money's all gone, and Papa won't give me a cent of allowance until next month. By that time, the ship will be gone because it's so beautiful someone is sure to buy it."

"Won't your mother buy it for you?" Elsie inquired.

"I asked, but she said she can't spare the money right now. It's so near the end of the month that we've all spent our allowances. Except Louise, but she says she won't lend money to a spendthrift like me."

Elsie took out her little purse and seemed ready to give it to Arthur. But she hesitated a moment, then returned it to her pocket. "Five dollars is a lot of money for a little girl like me," she said with a small smile. "I have to think about it, Arthur."

"I'm not asking you to *give* me money," Arthur contended. "I'll pay it back in two weeks."

Elsie only said, "Let me think about it until tomorrow morning," and she turned away from her disconsolate uncle. Arthur glanced at her retreating figure, and one angry word slipped from his lips: "Stingy."

But Elsie was still smiling as she ran down to the kitchen in search of Pompey, who was one of her special friends among the household servants. Finding him at last, she asked, "Pompey, are you going into the city tonight?"

"I am, Miss Elsie. I have some errands to do for Mrs. Dinsmore and the family, so I'll be leaving in about ten minutes. Is there something you want, eh?"

Elsie moved close and put her purse in Pompey's hand. Whispering, she told the old man about Arthur's wish and asked if he would take the money, and a half-dollar for his trouble, and purchase the coveted toy. And could he keep it secret from the others?

"I sure can do that," Pompey replied, a broad grin lighting his face. "I'll do this business just right for you."

— *Elsie's Endless Wait*, pages 33–34

*N*ow that we have learned about walking in love, joy, peace, and patience, we turn our attention to the fruit of kindness. The word "kindness," unlike the word "patience," makes people comfortable at the mere mention of it. Whether we are on the giving or the receiving end of kindness, kindness makes people feel good. And it often paves the way for other powerful works of the Holy Spirit.

In the above excerpt from *Elsie's Endless Wait*, we see the joy Elsie felt in planning to surprise Arthur with an act of kindness. As you may remember, Pompey did in fact purchase the boat that Arthur wanted and Elsie was able to surprise him with it the next morning. Arthur was thrilled! So thrilled in fact that he apologized to Elsie for teasing her and promised not to do it again. See how Elsie's act of kindness paved the way for a great work of the Holy Spirit—Arthur's humbling himself and actually apologizing!

Maybe you can't understand how Elsie could be so kind and considerate. Elsie walked in love, plain and simple. And from that love, whenever there was an opportunity, we see the fruit of the Spirit blossoming from her soul and displaying a fantastic kindness!

Yet as hard as it may seem to be so kind all the time, it really is not beyond the reach of any of us. Remember, the fruit of the Spirit is the fruit *of the Spirit* — it is not fruit *of us!* It is the life and power *of God* in you, not your own life and power. On your own, you cannot be something you are not. But in *His* power, you can be so much more than you ever dreamed. You can be everything He created you to be!

What exactly is kindness? In the space below, write your own definition.

List some ways that Elsie was kind to the people in her life.

**Kindness does not wait to be asked. It offers, without expecting anything in return. Kindness looks for places to help and needs to minister to.**

We often think of things like kindness, love, joy, peace, patience, goodness . . . as separate from each other. But when we try to develop one of them in our lives, we discover that they are all connected. For example, if we don't have joy, it's difficult to be kind, no matter how hard we may try. Kindness, like patience, is an inward state of heart. We can *do* a number of kind things for others, but unless our *hearts* are filled with kindness, our efforts amount to nothing more than *acts*. Sooner or later, it will be obvious that we are *acting*. However, when we remember the riches of God's kindness, which the apostle Paul reminds us of in Romans 2:4, our hearts are consumed by His love. From love, the rest follows.

# Other-Centered

> One afternoon, all the children were taking a walk — Arthur and Walter running far ahead because they would not accommodate Herbert's slow pace — when Herbert asked to stop and rest for awhile. "I want to try out my new bow, and you girls can pick up my arrows."
>
> "Thank you, sir," Lucy laughed. "Elsie can chase your arrows if she likes, but I plan to take a nap. This soft grass will make an elegant couch." And she dropped onto the ground and was soon slumbering soundly, or pretending to be. Herbert shot his arrows here and there, and Elsie ran to retrieve them until she was hot and breathless.
>
> "I have to rest," she said, sitting down beside Herbert. "What if I tell you a story?"
>
> "Please do," said Herbert, laying down his bow. "You know how much I like your stories."
>
> —*Elsie's Endless Wait*, pages 79–80

Herbert Carrington was near in age to Arthur and Walter and was a close friend and playmate. Yet notice in the above passage that when the children were out for a walk together, Arthur and Walter did not wait for their friend Herbert, who suffered from a bone disease that made him slower than the other children. Elsie, on the other hand, made it a point to play with Herbert until she was exhausted, and afterwards she told him a story.

What does this tell us about Elsie?

Read and think about the following Bible verses:

❖ "*Bear* with one another in love" (Ephesians 4:2).

❖ "*Serve* one another in love" (Galatians 5:13).

❖ "*Carry* each other's burdens" (Galatians 6:2).

❖ "Do not be proud, but *be willing to associate with* people in low position" (Romans 12:16).

❖ "*Share* with God's people who are in need" (Romans 12:13).

Notice all the italicized words. What do they have in common?

How did Elsie's kindness to Herbert demonstrate her love for Jesus?

*Kind acts come from a heart that is focused on other people.* In your own words, describe what you think it means to be "other-focused."

Before European explorers like Amerigo Vespucci and Christopher Columbus set sail to the Americas, people looked upon the expanse of ocean and believed that the Earth was flat. Because they had never sailed to the horizon's edge, they thought that surely if they did, they would fall from Earth. Maps, therefore, showed a fixed, central location and the areas extending out from it. However, even after the discovery of the new world and the revelation that the earth was in fact *round*—with no fixed, central location—countries still drew maps placing themselves not east nor west according to their latitudes, but dead center, as if their presence defined east and west for all the other nations, which was not true.

 **People tend to view themselves in the center of all life around them, as if their presence was the defining factor in all things.**

What is *your* "center?" In the spaces below, answer the following questions.

What, more than anything else, seems to occupy your thoughts on a daily basis?

If, today, you could have, do, or be anything you want, what would it be?

Do you think other people should pay more attention to *your* wants and needs?

Your responses to the above questions may show that the bulk of your time and attention is primarily invested in yourself. If so, you are not alone. Most of our lives are centered around ourselves!

 **God wants us to focus more of our attention on Him and on others, rather than always on ourselves. That is why the fruit of kindness is so important: kindness is *other*-centered. It focuses us outward and inspires us to be seeking ways to show God's love to other people.**

Elsie enjoyed meeting the needs of other people and showing them kindness in various ways. List several people in your life to whom you could be more kind and what you could do for them.

# Passion Turned Outward

"'Twas thinking about Arthur, Papa. I would like very much to give him a nice present before he goes away. May I?"

"If you wish," Horace replied.

"Thank you, Papa. I was half-afraid you wouldn't let me. Since I can't go shopping, will you buy the present for me the next time you go into the city? I'd like to give him the very best pocket Bible you can find. And I'd like for you to write his name inside, and mine, so he'll know it is a token of affection from me. Will you, Papa?"

"I will, dear, but I doubt Arthur will appreciate such a gift," Horace said gently.

"He might, Papa, if it is *very* handsomely bound," Elsie said, though her voice betrayed her own doubts. "I want to try anyway. When does Arthur leave, Papa?"

"The day after tomorrow."

"Do you think he might come and see me before he goes? I wish he would."

"I'll ask him," Horace promised. "But why do you want to see him after all the pain he has caused you?"

Elsie sighed deeply. "I want him to know that I'm not angry with him and that I feel so sorry he has to go away all alone to live with strangers."

By now, Horace was used to Elsie's ability to forgive, but her sympathy for Arthur still took him by surprise. "You need not waste your kind thoughts on him," Horace said a little hotly. "In fact, I think he rather likes the idea of going away to school."

Now it was Elsie's turn to be surprised, for nothing could frighten her more than the thought of being separated from her Papa. "He does?" she exclaimed. "How strange!"

True to his form, Arthur did refuse to see Elsie and even wanted to decline her gift. But when Lora suggested that he might need a Bible for his schoolwork and when he saw that the little book was indeed very handsome, he grudgingly accepted the present. But nothing could convince him to see Elsie, and when she sent him a gracious little note, he ignored her offer of friendship. And so Arthur departed from Roselands without any apology or even a sign that he regretted his behavior.

—*Elsie's Impossible Choice*, pages 89–90

Remember when Elsie heard that Arthur would be sent away to boarding school? She cried, "Oh, Papa, that's terrible! I can't think of anything worse than being sent away and having to live with strangers. Can't you ask Grandpa to forgive him this time? Must he be sent away?"

Even though Arthur had tormented her relentlessly, Elsie never thought of being rid of him. She possessed a heart of compassion. She wanted for Arthur the very things that she would want for herself. And the things that would cause her pain, she never wanted to see anyone else suffer. Such was Elsie's love that she grieved at the thought that Arthur had to leave against his will.

The Bible encourages us to "mourn with those who mourn," and not only that, but to "rejoice with those who rejoice" (Romans 12:15). Compassion feels deeply the joys and losses of others. And that's why compassion best sums up the inward state of kindness.

The fruit of kindness is genuine. It is long lasting and runs deep. Sometimes we think of compassion as merely a fleeting moment when we identify with the hardships of others and say something to the effect of, "Oh, isn't it terrible that this tragedy has happened to them?" We might even shed a few tears, but we move on. Compassion, though, is born of God. Instead of expressing kindness or concern and then moving on, it doesn't move on; compassion *moves out* and *moves in!*

Because compassion or the fruit of kindness is other-centered, it always looks for needs to meet. The word compassion literally means "with passion." The fruit of kindness cannot be put to rest while another is hurting. On the contrary, it weeps with those who weep . . . it bears with others . . . it helps carry the burdens of others.

Compassion demands *action*. James 2:15–16 asks, "Suppose a brother or sister is without clothes and daily food. If one of you says to him, 'Go, I wish you well; keep warm and well fed,' but does nothing about his physical condition, what good is it?" What does this verse tell us about how to be kind to others?

As children of God, we have an obligation to help the poor of our community, country, and world. Taking into account your age and situation, what are some practical things that you can do to help those in need of physical things? (Be creative!)

Kindness, let's not forget, includes much more than helping to meet physical needs. List other things — such as time, a smile, listening to someone, etc. — that you have to give. Be specific.

# No Favorites

> Horace [unlike Elsie] had no such place of refuge and peace, yet his struggle was every bit as difficult as Elsie's. More difficult, in fact, because Horace had been cruelly misled by someone who had neither his interests nor his daughter's in her heart.
>
> Mrs. Dinsmore could not be accused of slighting Horace's physical care. She was an excellent nurse, attending to all her patient's needs during his long illness. Indeed, Doctor Barton credited her in good measure for Horace's survival, and even Aunt Chloe had seen Mrs. Dinsmore push aside her own exhaustion to stay at Horace's side day and night throughout his fever and until his recovery was assured.
>
> But Mrs. Dinsmore's good deeds only masked her jealous heart. She had always resented Horace, the stepson who caused so much trouble in his youth yet rated so highly in his father's esteem. When Horace had been sent away to college — after his early marriage and before the birth of his child — Mrs. Dinsmore had secretly welcomed his departure from Roselands. Then, just when she thought that Horace might never trouble her again, his daughter had appeared like an orphan on the doorstep, and all of Mrs. Dinsmore's bitter resentment had been turned upon the child.
>
> —*Elsie's Impossible Choice*, pages 127–128

Imagine that it's the first day of a new school year. Seated at your desk, you watch as classmates trickle in and take their seats. There is a seat available right next to you. Three girls come in. One is someone who you don't get along with. Another is a new, shy girl dressed in old-fashioned clothes. The last girl to come in is the most popular girl in school. Of these three girls, who do you want to sit next to you and why?

Now, read James 2:1-4 for a similar example.

Whether in conscious thoughts, or somewhere deep within us, we all make judgments. Though they begin as secret thoughts that we never intend to make known, they become obvious in our behavior.

**How we act toward others as each day passes can steer the course of our whole lives.**

The apostle James wrote, "My brothers, as believers in our glorious Lord Jesus Christ, *don't show favoritism*" (James 2:1). What is "favoritism?"

Generally, we want to be with people that we favor. When we think of the unfavored (the "uncool"), we do not want to be with them.

*Favoritism focuses on the flaws in others. Like unforgiveness, it judges against people, rather than accepting them in the love of Jesus.* Favoritism chooses based on its own pleasures and desires. Love, on the other hand, does not seek personal gain or pleasure.

Unfortunately, the world has little concept of what love really means. Through His life . . . upon His death . . . and in His Word, Jesus defines love. The apostle John writes, "*This is love*: not that we have loved God, but that he loved us and sent his Son as an atoning sacrifice for our sins" (1 John 4:10). This verse shows us that *love is not merely responding to those who love us. Rather, it is an overwhelming desire to care for or promote the well-being of people — whether they love us or not.* Love is willing to sacrifice its greatest treasures, its wants, its time, for the benefit of others.

How does judging others prevent us from experiencing the fruit of the Holy Spirit in our lives?

James asks us, "Has not God chosen those who are poor [or unpopular] in the eyes of the world to be rich in faith?" (v. 5). With this question, he attempts to remind us that God possesses an entirely different standard of measure. Wealth . . . popularity . . . attractiveness . . . style . . . things that appear of value in the eyes of the world, have no meaning to Him. He cautions us, "Do not love the world or anything in the world," because our lust for those things will blind us to His heart and the needs of His people.

Do you think that Elsie differentiated between slaves like Aunt Chloe and free people like Mrs. Murray, or between friends like Miss Allison and foes like Arthur? Why or why not?

It seemed that Elsie loved many people, and the only time she judged was occasionally to examine *her own heart* before the Lord.

The Gospel of Luke encourages us, "Do not judge, and you will not be judged. Do not condemn, and you will not be condemned. Forgive, and you will be forgiven. Give, and it will be given to you" (Luke 6:37).

# Kind to the Unkind

As Elsie lay on the sofa, she seemed almost her old self. The color had come back to her face, and although her leg hurt badly, she was smiling at her father.

"Tell me how you fell, dear," Horace urged.

"Must I, Papa? I'd rather not," she pleaded.

Horace was too grateful to have his daughter safe to push for an answer, so he let the matter drop. Besides, he was sure he already knew the cause of her injury.

When the ankle had been wrapped and instructions given for Elsie's care, the doctor remarked kindly on her patience and courage before he rose to leave. At the front door, however, he paused to say one more thing to Horace alone. "That's a sweet child, you have," he began. "I don't see how anyone could want to harm her. But believe me, Horace, there has been foul play somewhere. She did not fall without help. I would get to the bottom of it, if I were you."

—*Elsie's Impossible Choice*, pages 68–69

Arthur pushed Elsie down a ravine. He repeatedly sabotaged her schoolwork. He allowed her to be falsely accused . . . and falsely punished. He alienated and instigated, teased and tormented. But can you think of one instance when Elsie returned evil for evil? Can you recall a single word spoken, or even a glance given with malicious intent? Was there ever a time when Elsie so much as expressed a desire to hurt Arthur? *Elsie, through the strength that God gave her, never sought revenge.*

Those who knew Elsie could not deny that she was kind — astonishingly so. In fact, those without the Holy Spirit ridiculed her as *abnormally* kind! But Elsie loved the Lord and loved His Word. And because she loved Him, she could do no less than love others!

**Elsie's love for Jesus did not give her the option to hate.**

Among other things, Elsie knew God's Word, which says, "Do not repay anyone evil for evil. Be careful to do what is right in the eyes of everybody. *If it is possible, as far as it depends on you, live at peace with everyone.* Do not take revenge, my friends, but leave room for God's wrath, for it is written: 'It is Mine to avenge; I will repay,' says the Lord'" (Romans 12:17–19).

When someone hurts us, a desire wells up within us to hurt them back. Giving in to that desire leads us to take revenge. Revenge is an act to satisfy ourselves, to stop our pain.

To whom do the above verses say revenge belongs?

Second Thessalonians 1:6–7 tells us, "God is just: He will pay back trouble to those who trouble you, and give relief to you who are troubled." There is no need to take matters into our own hands. God will deal with those who have hurt us. It is in His hands, not ours!

As the eternal Judge, God alone has the rights to retribution. Retribution simply means to repay someone for what they have done. When we're hurt, or when someone has disappointed us, it takes faith to believe that God sees everything, that He judges His people, and that He will correct those who have harmed us. *To resist taking revenge is, therefore, an act of faith.* We believe in a God who actively defends justice, who protects and defends all His people.

When we take revenge against someone, what do our actions reveal about our trust in our heavenly Father?

Did Jesus ever take revenge against anyone?

Sometimes we get back at the person who has hurt or wronged us through subtle or indirect ways that do not openly appear to be revenge. It's easy to disguise our revenge so that even we (and others) might not be aware that we are trying to hurt someone. To illustrate this, look at the list below. How do you respond when someone hurts or wrongs you? Circle or check any of the following behaviors that apply to you:

❏ pouting/giving the silent treatment

❏ giving hurtful looks

❏ holding a grudge

❏ gossiping

❏ refusing to look at the person

❏ saying hurtful words

❏ other: _____

❏ withholding compliments

❏ withdrawing friendship

❏ name-calling

❏ withholding courtesy

❏ withdrawing from others

❏ purposely acting hurt so that others will notice

Often we try to excuse these behaviors, saying that they were not willful choices but just expressions of our pain. *But God never permits deliberate attempts to hurt others.* Quite the opposite, His Word commands us, "Do not seek revenge or bear a grudge against one of your people, but love your neighbor as yourself" (Leviticus 19:18).

Remember what we learned earlier in *Elsie's Life Lessons* about how to treat our enemies? The Word of God tells us, "If your enemy is hungry, feed him; if he is thirsty, give him something to drink . . . . Do not be overcome by evil, but overcome evil with good" (Romans 12:20, 21). This will not usually be easy. It takes the help of the Holy Spirit. But it is possible through the fruit of kindness.

List some people that you can think of that have hurt or wronged you and that you are holding some bad feelings against.

What are some practical ways that you can return kindness to them?

Look back over this chapter. Ask the Holy Spirit to show you the most important things He wants you to remember. Put a star beside those truths and, in your own words, summarize below what He showed you.

Rewrite your thoughts as a prayer, asking God to help you grow and apply the truths He's taught you throughout the chapter.

Write out the memory verse for this chapter:

Write out Galatians 5:22–23, the memory verse for our entire study guide:

CHAPTER

6

# *Walking in Goodness*

### Lesson 1
*More Than "Nice-ness"*

### Lesson 2
*A Light in a Dark World*

### Lesson 3
*Motives of the Heart*

### Lesson 4
*The Darkness of Dishonesty*

### Lesson 5
*A Defense Against Temptation*

# *Walking in Goodness*

**by heart**

Dear friends, I urge you, as aliens and strangers in the world, to abstain from sinful desires, which war against your soul. Live such good lives among the pagans that, though they accuse you of doing wrong, they may see your good deeds and glorify God on the day he visits us.

—1 PETER 2:11–12

## More Than "Nice-ness"

"What are you thinking about?" Horace asked Elsie at length.

"A good many things, Papa. I was thinking of what you said and how glad I am to know that you truly love me. And I was asking God to help us both to do His will. And I thought that I might be able to always do what you bid, without disobeying Him. May I say my lesson now? I think I know it perfectly."

"Of course," he said in an abstracted way.

Elsie brought the Bible to him and drew up a stool for herself beside his chair. With her arm over his knee, she began to repeat with great feeling the chapters she had learned — the touching description of the Last Supper and Jesus' farewell to His sorrowing disciples.

"Isn't it beautiful, Papa?" she asked when she had finished her recitation. "'Having loved His own who were in the world, he now showed them the full extent of His love,'" she quoted again.

"It seems so strange that Jesus could be so thoughtful of them when all the time He knew the dreadful death He was going to die. And He knew they were all going to run away and leave Him to His enemies. It's so sweet to know that Jesus is so loving and that He loves me and will love me forever."

"But do you think you are good enough for Jesus to love you?" Horace asked.

"I know I'm not at all good, Papa," she said with grave seriousness. "My thoughts and feelings are often wrong, and Jesus knows all about it. But that doesn't keep Him from loving me because it was sinners He died to save. How good and kind He is. And who could help loving Him?"

—*Elsie's Endless Wait*, pages 182–183

In the above excerpt from *Elsie's Endless Wait*, Horace asked Elsie if she thought she was "good enough" for Jesus to love her. Elsie told her father that she knew she was *not* good enough. "My thoughts and feelings are often wrong, and Jesus knows all about it. But that doesn't keep Him from loving me because it was sinners He died to save," responded Elsie.

Jesus taught in Mark 10:18, "No one is good — except God alone." *True goodness resides in God alone and is not possible apart from Him.*

There is a hard reality that all of us need to grasp: as humans, we are not and can never be "good enough" to please God and earn His love. God is perfect and holy — *completely pure and without sin.* Because we sin, we fall short of His standards.

To "sin" is to break one of God's laws or rules. You might not think of yourself as a "sinner." But because of the sin of Adam and Eve, you (along with all human beings) were born with a sinful nature already inside of you. You might not have committed "big" sins like murder, but at times you have, no doubt, committed lots of "little" sins, like being mean, selfish, disobedient, impatient, untruthful, ungrateful, or unkind, or you may have done other things that are wrong in God's eyes. *For it is God, not man, who determines what is right and what is wrong.* Whether a person's sins are big or little doesn't really matter because everything that falls short of God's standards is sin.

There is no way we can erase or make up for our sins, no matter how many good deeds we do. But the good news is that God Himself came up with a way to cancel the punishment due for the sins He holds against you! In His great love, God sent His Son Jesus to bear the punishment for your sins and for the sins of all human beings.

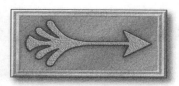

**It is the sinlessness of Jesus that makes us good enough in God's eyes.**

When we have asked Jesus to come into our hearts and His Holy Spirit lives within us, we become clothed with the righteousness of Christ, like a garment. When God looks at us, He sees us wrapped in this garment of His Son's holiness and we become acceptable in His sight. Because His Holy Spirit dwells in us, all the fruit of the Holy Spirit, including goodness, are available to us.

Write your own definition of "goodness" here.

Most people think of goodness as being "nice," but goodness goes farther than that. *Many of us can be nice apart from God; but goodness is a quality far superior and beyond our reach without the Holy Spirit.* You can be nice for a variety of reasons, including selfish reasons (for example, when you do it because you want something from someone). But true goodness arises from a genuine purity and is uncorrupted by such impure motives. Goodness is a purity and uprightness of heart and life that is reflected in honesty, right motives, truth, and decency.

While many of the people around Elsie might have seen her "goodness" as coming from her, she saw it as *coming from Jesus!* Elsie tried to be like Jesus, and she knew that *it was only by the power of His Holy Spirit within her that she could exhibit any true goodness at all.*

When we think of goodness, we often think of good deeds. As we will see, good deeds are an important aspect of goodness, but they are not the whole story because, like the other dimensions of the fruit of the Holy Spirit, *goodness is a matter of the heart.* Perhaps that is why Luke 6:45 tells us, "The good man brings good things *out of the good stored up in his heart.*"

 **Since goodness begins in the heart, the state of our hearts is very important.**

Take a moment now to ask the Holy Spirit to examine your heart and show you if there is anything in it that is hindering His goodness from flowing in and through you. Write down what He reveals to you.

In Ephesians 2:10, we read, "For we are God's workmanship, created in Christ Jesus to do good works, which God prepared in advance for us to do."

What do you think the relationship is between goodness (purity and uprightness of heart) and good works?

Our memory verse for this chapter, 1 Peter 2:11–12, also speaks of good works. Write out 1 Peter 2:11–12 here.

Good works are the same as good deeds. According to our memory verse, who is watching the good deeds we do and why does it matter?

Can you think of a good deed that you saw someone else do (either for you or for somebody else) that caused you to give praise to God? If so, describe it here and explain why you praised God for it.

# A Light in a Dark World

As the other girls bounded merrily from the room, Elsie slowly approached her father, who had seated himself on the sofa to read his newspaper. Becoming aware of her approach, he asked, "What is it, Daughter?"

In spite of her best efforts, tears gathered in her eyes and a bright flush rose to her cheeks. "Oh, Papa," she said in a hesitating voice. "Please don't be angry with me. I didn't know that you cared so much for my curls, and I gave one to Carrie for her mother's bracelet. I didn't think about them belonging to you."

Horace was very much surprised by this outburst, but his tone was gentle: "No, dearest, I won't be angry this time. I understand that you didn't know how much I care about everything that affects you — even your pretty curls."

Elsie's relief was enormous. "I'll never do it again, Papa. I promise," she said with intensity. "But I know you must punish me. I was afraid to tell you at first because I thought you wouldn't let me go riding with you."

> Horace searched her face. "Then why didn't you delay your confession until after our ride?" he questioned. Elsie had begun to tremble again, but her father's voice was kind and reassuring.
>
> Elsie blushed. "I wanted to wait, Papa, but I knew that would be wrong."
>
> Horace gathered her in his arms and said, "Dear Elsie, I am proud of you for your honesty and truthfulness. You have done what is right, and I'd never think of punishing you for that.
>
> —*Elsie's Impossible Choice*, pages 53–54

*I*n what way did Elsie exhibit "goodness" in the above passage?

The timing of Elsie's confession surprised her father and probably would have surprised others because most people would have either delayed their confession until after the ride or not confessed at all. What would you have done? (Be honest.)

Does Elsie's unusual truthfulness make you uncomfortable at all? Why or why not?

Listen to how Elsie was described in *Elsie's Endless Wait*:

> Young as Elsie was, she already had a well-developed Christian character. Though not remarkably precocious in other respects, she seemed to have very clear and correct views on her duty to God and her neighbor. She was truthful in both word and deed, very strict in her observation of the Sabbath — unlike the rest of the Dinsmore family — diligent in her studies, respectful to her elders, polite and kind to everyone. She was gentle, sweet-tempered, patient, and forgiving to a remarkable degree.
>
> —Elsie's Endless Wait, page 30

Through her words and actions, the radiance of the Holy Spirit shined brightly through Elsie. The light she reflected occasionally made others uncomfortable, but whether people were comfortable or not — whether they were encouraged or convicted of their sin — the light that shined through Elsie came from God!

As we read in the above excerpt, Elsie was "unlike" the rest of the Dinsmore family. When Jesus walked this earth, He was considered unlike (different from) others too. He was *in* our world, but certainly not *of it*. If we are truly following Him, it's safe to assume that we will be considered "different" as well. People will think there is something unusual about us.

Does your desire to love and please God cause you to behave and respond differently from others? If so, in what ways are you different? List as many as you can think of.

How do you feel about being different? Do you like it, or does it make you uncomfortable? Is it difficult sometimes? Write your thoughts below and then take a moment, and tell your heavenly Father about your feelings.

As carriers of the Holy Spirit, filled with the light of salvation, each of us becomes a beacon of that light! We may never preach the Gospel before a gathering or set our feet on foreign soil to evangelize unreached peoples, but right where we live, our Father has called us to glorify His Son each and every day of our lives—to serve as a lighthouse.

 **As children of the light, our calling is to reflect God's light in a dark world.**

Jesus said, "As My Father has sent me, I am sending you" (John 20:21). Then in Matthew 5:14 he says, "You are the light of the world." He goes on to tell us, "A city on a hill cannot be hidden. Neither do people light a lamp and put it under a bowl. Instead, they put it on its stand, and it gives light to everyone in the house. In the same way, let your light shine before men, that they may see your good deeds and praise your Father in heaven" (Matthew 5:14–16).

Does the phrase "that they may see your good deeds and praise your Father in heaven" remind you of a part of our memory verse? If so, write out that part here.

Elsie lived as a light and her life made a difference. In what ways do you live as a light and see your life making an impact?

# Motives of the Heart

Had Elsie been ugly, Mrs. Dinsmore might have shown more sympathy, for she always found pleasure in looking down on the less fortunate. But Elsie was a lovely child who would become a beautiful woman. It didn't help that Elsie was an heiress who would someday have wealth far beyond anything Mrs. Dinsmore's own daughters could hope for. Most important, Elsie was gifted with a gentle temperament and instinctive kindness that were foreign to Mrs. Dinsmore's understanding. With poisonous, little words — "so meek and spineless," "so lacking the Dinsmore strength of character," "such a rigid little Christian" — Mrs. Dinsmore had gradually succeeded in turning her husband against the child, and she encouraged her own children to taunt and tease the little intruder. Her own unfair and even abusive attitude was apparent to everyone except her husband.

Horace's return to Roselands had put an end to Mrs. Dinsmore's open campaign against Elsie, but the woman did not cease looking for opportunities to undermine the child's new position in her father's affections.

—*Elsie's Impossible Choice*, page 128

In the above passage, we get a glimpse into the heart of Mrs. Dinsmore. With hidden motives, like the serpent in the Garden, Mrs. Dinsmore sowed doubt and distrust and bitter poison in her plot against Elsie. What do you think Mrs. Dinsmore's motive was?

The Bible tells us that the Lord *searches every heart* and *understands every motive* (1 Chronicles 28:9). And in Proverbs 16:2, we read, "All a man's ways seem innocent to him, but motives are weighed by the Lord." Those verses tell us that the secret places of the heart are what matter, and they are *clearly visible to God.*

In Psalm 139:23–24, David prayed, "Search me, O God, and know my *heart* . . . See if there is any offensive way in me, and lead me in the way everlasting." And in Psalm 51:10, he asked for God to create in him a "clean heart."

What do you think it means to have a "clean heart?"

As we discovered when we looked at Elsie earlier, purity of motive and uprightness of heart are essential to goodness and will cause us to shine God's light in the darkness.

**In the kingdom of God, light and darkness exist as rivals. Jesus, we know, is the Light of the world, but Satan is the prince of darkness.**

In the Book of Ephesians, we're told, "Have nothing to do with the fruitless deeds of darkness, but rather expose them . . . . Everything exposed by the light becomes visible, for it is light that makes everything visible" (Ephesians 5:11, 13–14). Sin, deception, deceit, and lies — these come from the darkness. When we hide the truth from ourselves or from others — when we deny or justify our sin — we surrender control of that area of our lives to the power of darkness. Tragically, the fruit of darkness is evil.

If the fruit of darkness is evil, what do you think the fruit of light is?

We know from God's Word that because Jesus is the Light of the world, His light has the power to expose all things. He has assured us, "There is nothing concealed that will not be disclosed, or hidden that will not be made known. What you have said in the dark will be heard in the daylight, and what you have whispered in the ear in the inner rooms will be proclaimed from the roofs" (Luke 12:2–3).

What do you suppose sin's worst nightmare is?

If you guessed "light," you're absolutely correct! Light brings sin out into the open where it is exposed. Without a hiding place, it loses its power. Darkness is powerful . . . but light is invincible!

How does confessing our sin introduce light into the darkness?

In what way does reading the Bible shine the light of God into our hearts and expose the darkness?

Can you think of a time where your reading the Bible exposed some darkness in you? If so, describe it here.

# The Darkness of Dishonesty

"All this time on one little problem?" Arthur replied with a sneering laugh. "You ought to be ashamed, Elsie Dinsmore. Why, I could have done it a half a dozen times before now."

"Well, I've been over it and over it," Elsie said sadly, "and there are still two numbers that won't come out right."

"How do you know they're not right, little miss?" Arthur asked, grabbing at her curls as he spoke.

"Please don't pull my hair!" she cried. Then she explained that she had the correct answer, so she knew that her answer was wrong.

"Then why not just write down the right numbers?" Arthur asked. "That's what I'd do."

"But that wouldn't be honest."

"Nonsense! Nobody will know if you cheat a little."

"It would be like telling a lie," Elsie said firmly, then sighed and put aside her slate. "But I'll never get it right with you bothering me."

Elsie tried to turn her attention to her geography book, but Arthur would not stop his persecutions. He tickled her, pulled at her hair, flipped the book out of her hands, and kept up his incessant chatter and questions. On the verge of tears, Elsie begged him once again to leave her to her lessons.

"Take your book out on the veranda, Elsie, and study there," said Louise. "I'll call you when Miss Day comes back."

But Elsie did not budge from her desk. "I can't go outside because Miss Day said we must stay in this room, so that would be disobeying," she explained with despair.

Giving up on the geography, she took her copybook and pen and ink from her desk. She dipped her pen into the ink and very carefully formed every letter on the clean, white paper. But Arthur stood over her as she wrote, criticizing every letter she made. At last, he jogged her elbow, and all the ink in her pen dropped onto the paper, making a large black blot.

It was too much, and Elsie burst into tears. "Now I won't get to ride to the fair! Miss Day will never let me go! And I wanted so much to see the beautiful flowers."

Arthur, who was not always as hateful as he seemed, felt suddenly guilty about the mischief he had caused. "Never mind, Elsie. I can fix it," he said. "I'll just tear out this page with the ink stain, and you can start again on the next page. I won't bother you anymore, and I can help with your arithmetic problem, too."

Elsie smiled at him through her tears. "That's kind of you, Arthur, but I can't tear out the page or let you do my problem. That would be deceitful."

—*Elsie's Endless Wait*, pages 5–7

When something is deceitful, it is intended to mislead. We can purposely tell a lie, or we can give the wrong impression by dividing the truth and only telling a part of it.

*Elsie understood what deceitfulness and dishonesty were and she wanted no part of them.* Second Corinthians 11:14 warns of those who attempt to cloak (or cover) deception in light. It tells us that "Satan himself masquerades as an angel of light."

What was it that gave Elsie the strength to resist temptations to be dishonest or deceitful?

Have you ever been dishonest or deceitful? If so, take some time right now to confess your sin to the Lord and ask Him to forgive you. This is very important.

Truthfulness in our lives reflects the purity of goodness in our hearts. Jesus declared, "I am the way and the *truth* and the life" (John 14:6).

 **When the truth of the Lord shows in us through the fruit of goodness, it will point other people to Jesus!**

Remember when Elsie was about to be punished for her messy copybook when she wasn't to blame? At the last moment, just as Horace was about to punish Elsie, Lora burst into the room and cried urgently for Horace not to punish Elsie because she just *knew* Elsie could not be guilty. Horace asked her how she could be so sure, and Lora's response was as follows:

> "In the first place," Lora began, "there is Elsie's established character for truthfulness. In all the time she has been with us, she has always been perfectly truthful in word and deed. And what motive would she have for spoiling her own book? She knew that your punishment was certain to be very severe. Horace, I'm sure Arthur is at the bottom of this. He won't confess, but he doesn't deny it. And I saw Elsie's book just yesterday. It was neat and well written and had absolutely no blots."
>
> "Thank you, dear Lora, for stopping me before I punished Elsie unfairly. I need no more than your word to establish her innocence."
>
> —*Elsie's Endless Wait*, page 162

How did Elsie's "established character for truthfulness" protect her in this situation?

How did Elsie's consistently telling the truth in the past reflect goodness to the people around her?

Would your friends and family say that you *consistently* tell the truth?

# A Defense Against Temptation

Such temptation! Elsie could see that the package contained all her favorite candies and treats, and she would dearly have loved to taste each and every one of them. But her Papa was very strict about what she ate and had instructed her never to take candy of any kind unless he gave his express permission. Though she wanted to accept the gift, Elsie had to say, politely, "Thank you very much, Miss Stevens, but Papa has told me not to take candy from anyone. He does not approve of children eating sweets." Miss Stevens pouted. "That's too bad," she said, "but surely you can have one or two pieces, at least. They are really delicious, and they can't possibly hurt you. Your father need never know."

Elsie was surprised by this offer. "But Miss Stevens," she said, "God would know, and I would know. How could I look at my Papa if I deceived him?"

*—Elsie's Impossible Choice*, pages 39–40

Elsie's love for her father and for God enabled her to resist many forms of temptation. She knew that they wanted what was best for her and she trusted them.

When something we are asked to do is contrary to our standards of rightness or righteousness, we need to reject it. Goodness inside our hearts protects us by giving us a standard for truth—a standard by which we can discern or recognize wickedness. Because goodness knows what is right according to God's truth, goodness will guard us. This makes goodness something we should treasure, nurture, and protect. Without it, wickedness could easily sneak in and subtly lead us astray.

The first part of our memory verse, 1 Peter 2:11, says, "Dear friends, I urge you, as aliens and strangers in the world, to abstain from sinful desires, which war against your soul." Christians are referred to as "aliens and strangers in this world" because of what we discussed before about our being "different" from those around us. One of the things that makes Christians so different is that they abstain (or stay away from and want no part of) the sinful desires of this world. Sinful desires are desires that go against what God would want for us.

How can we protect ourselves from the assaults of sinful desires?

Temptations can come in all sorts of shapes and sizes! In the above excerpt, Elsie was tempted to eat candy when her father had forbidden it. Earlier in our study guide, we read about Arthur tempting her to lie and cheat.

What kind of temptations do *you* face regularly? List them below in terms of the different areas of your life: At home—with parents, responsibilities, and siblings; at school—with teachers and peers; and alone.

## TEMPTATIONS AT HOME

## TEMPTATIONS AT SCHOOL

## TEMPTATIONS WHEN ALONE

If we were to look at temptations more closely, we would see that there is a reason they appeal to us: temptations offer us something we want. However, that something might not be something that is good for us. *Or it might be something good for us, but it is offered to us in a wrong or bad way.* Let's study some temptations and see what we can learn.

From the temptations you face listed on the previous page, choose some of them and see if you can fill in the chart below. List the type of temptation and then write down why it appeals to you. Then see if you can identify a need or fear you have behind that reason.

| Type of Temptation | Reason Why it is Appealing | Underlying Need or Fear |
|---|---|---|
| temptation to gossip | I want to gain the acceptance of others | need to be liked |
| temptation to lie | I want to protect myself | fear that I will be punished |
|  |  |  |
|  |  |  |
|  |  |  |
|  |  |  |
|  |  |  |

After working through the temptations in the chart above, you will see that behind many temptations is often a need or a fear. In other words, because you need or fear something, it opens you up to offers to satisfy that need or resolve that fear. The problem is that most of these offers are not good or from God. *Rather than trusting in the promises of God, temptation leads us to doubt that God will come through.* As a result, we attempt to get satisfaction in our own way. This is *very* dangerous.

**To combat temptation, we must be strong in our faith. We must trust God to meet our needs and resolve our fears IN HIS WAY.**

To protect ourselves when tempted, we must choose the right thing we already know in our heart that we are supposed to do and immediately say "no" to that inner "voice" trying to convince us to sin. When tempted, we can call upon God for strength. He wants to help us!

**To keep from falling prey to sin, we must seal off the "openings" that allow it to gain entrance into our hearts. We do that by filling ourselves up with God's Word and by trusting that His boundaries — the guidelines and principles set forth in the Bible — are there to protect us.**

First Timothy 6:6 suggests still another thing that will help us ward off temptation. It says, "godliness with *contentment* is great gain." What does contentment have to do with temptation, you might ask.

**Lack of contentment leaves us open to temptation.**

First Timothy 6 goes on to say, "People who *want* . . . fall into temptation and a trap and into many foolish and harmful desires that plunge men into ruin and destruction." That's a pretty strong warning! But what it tells us is that *wanting something that is not good for you can ultimately lead to your destruction.*

God created us with needs and desires, so it is normal for us to have "wants." But in God's perfect plan, all our wants and desires are satisfied through Him and the things He provides. We have a choice. We can *trust God* the way a small child trusts in a loving mother and father for every need to be met. Or we can choose to *meet our own needs*, which causes us to disobey, manipulate, deceive, or fall prey to bad things, in order to get things to go our way.

Have you ever asked your parents for something, and when they responded by saying "No", you found it impossible to resist pleading, nagging, or hounding them? What do you think prompts this type of behavior by you?

How does this behavior undermine or weaken the ability of both your parents and God to protect you?




Very early on in her relationship with her Papa, Elsie learned not to nag her father. Although it was not easy for her at first, Elsie came to see that her Papa wanted what was best for her. Even more importantly, however, she knew that God wanted what was best for her. Somehow, even as a little girl, Elsie understood that God's rules were there to protect her. The boundaries set by God and our parents are there for our protection, not to deprive us of something good. We must learn to respect and obey those boundaries!

You might think that all the Bible's commands and strong warnings against sin are pretty severe, maybe even too harsh for a girl like you. Perhaps your sins and temptations seem small and insignificant—maybe only occasionally sneaking an extra cookie or cheating on schoolwork once or twice. *But it is the giving in to even small temptations that starts unhealthy patterns and bad habits in our lives.*

For example, have you ever eaten something utterly delicious? It was so good that you were tempted to eat more . . . and more . . . and more. Before you knew it, the treat was gone and you were sick to your stomach. This is what temptations do. They grow! You only wanted one taste, but you ate the whole box!

So, how can we resist these temptations? How did Elsie do it? Elsie trusted her father. But even more than that, Elsie chose to find her contentment through her relationship with the Lord. She trusted in the lovingkindness of God and looked to Him to satisfy her needs and desires and to resolve her fears. And because of her love relationship with God and constant study of His Word, she allowed the Holy Spirit to grow the fruit of goodness in her. With the fruit of goodness residing in her heart, she had internal standards—standards that came from God. They formed an important guard against temptation, and they helped her watch over her heart.

On a one to ten scale, with ten being the most content, how would you rate your level of contentment?

In what areas do you feel discontent?




Can you think of any unhealthy, unsafe, or ungodly ways you have tried to satisfy your own needs and wants (such as overeating)? If so, take some time now to talk to the Lord about it and ask Him to help you find healthy, safe and godly ways to meet those needs and wants.

Look back over this chapter. Ask the Holy Spirit to show you the most important things He wants you to remember. Put a star beside those truths and, in your own words, summarize below what He showed you.

Rewrite your thoughts as a prayer, asking God to help you grow and apply the truths He's taught you throughout the chapter.

Write out the memory verse for this chapter:

Write out Galatians 5:22–23, the memory verse for our entire study guide:

# CHAPTER

**7**

# Walking in Faithfulness

### Lesson 1
*Faithful and True*

### Lesson 2
*Firmly Committed to God's Word*

### Lesson 3
*Faithful in Times of Testing*

### Lesson 4
*Faithful in Prayer*

### Lesson 5
*Faithful to God's Will*

# Walking in Faithfulness

Let love and faithfulness never leave you; bind them around your neck, write them on the tablet of your heart. Then you will win favor and a good name in the sight of God and man.

— Proverbs 3:3–4

## Faithful and True

Elsie was torn. Her father's words promised a virtual paradise on earth. But the alternative! To be sent away into the care of strangers who could not be expected to love her or be sympathetic to her faith. (She was convinced that her father, in his determination to root out her beliefs, would select a boarding school where God was a stranger.) It was too terrible to consider. But if she chose what her heart longed for — to be restored to her father's affection — she must betray her higher duty and pledge to accept her father's commands over God's. Did ever a child face such a dreadful decision?

Quickly she found her Bible and turned to the book of Isaiah. There! There were the words she remembered: "I, even I, am He who comforts you. Who are you that you fear mortal men, the sons of men, who are but grass, that you forget the Lord your Maker, who stretched out the heavens and laid the foundations of the earth."

She could not forget her Maker; she could never abandon the One who loved and sustained her every hour and minute and second of her life. "I need not fear the consequences of following the commands of the Lord," she said to herself with fresh determination. "But help me to be strong, Lord Jesus. Please help me to be strong."

She closed the little book, and with her strength renewed, she left her room and went to meet Mrs. Dinsmore.

—*Elsie's Impossible Choice*, pages 176–177

One thing that Elsie seemed to be absolutely sure of was that God loved her. Day after day, year after year, Elsie had learned throughout her difficult and lonely childhood that God was *faithful* and His love was something she could *always* count on.

Lamentations 3:21–23 says, "Yet this I call to mind and therefore I have hope: Because of the Lord's great love we are not consumed, for his compassions never fail. They are new every morning; great is your faithfulness."

God's compassions *never* fail! They are new *every* morning! Think about that. So faithful is our God that each and every day of our lives — for *all* of our lives — from the beginning of time through the end of time, with each rising of the sun, a brand new day greets us to usher in new mercies for our lives from God! That's faithfulness beyond our wildest dreams! Regardless of our sin, our repeated failings, even our unfaithfulness, God remains perfectly, wonderfully loyal, forgiving and faithful. Not once, not twice, not fifty times, but every single day He grants us *new* mercies and another chance at a fresh start!

Webster's College Dictionary defines the word "faithfulness" as steady in allegiance or affection; loyal; constant; reliable; strict or thorough in the performance of a duty; true to a standard. Faithfulness speaks of *steadfast commitment*. You might say it gives us "staying power."

Write out the memory verse for this chapter, Proverbs 3:3–4.

The Lord wants us to walk in love and faithfulness to Him. What do you think it means to "bind them around your neck, write them on the tablet of your heart"?

All of us want our family and friends to love us and remain faithful to us. Do you have faithful friends? If so, describe how you know they are faithful.

A faithful friend believes the best about the one she loves. Regardless of faults and flaws, a faithful friend understands. She loves you for who you are, not what you do. A faithful friend doesn't let the "bad" in you cancel out the "good," but chooses to believe in you even when your good side isn't showing—*especially* when it isn't showing! A faithful friend stays around you even after you have "blown it."

How do you respond to your friends when things don't go your way? Do you prove to be committed to them, showing yourself to be a faithful friend? King Solomon once said: "Many a man claims to have unfailing love, but a faithful man who can find?" (Proverbs 20:6).

We can easily fool ourselves into thinking that we're more faithful than we are. *We tend to view ourselves as faithful while neglecting to consider that we're usually faithful only when our friends are "good."* If our friends should hurt us or treat us unfairly, that's an entirely different matter. When we are wronged or hurt, without so much as batting an eye, we justify treating them poorly or even ending the friendship. This is not true faithfulness. Faithfulness causes us to stay in the relationship even if difficulties sometimes arise.

List some individuals in your life to whom you should be faithful.

How have you shown faithfulness to them in the past?

List some friends that you gave up on (were unfaithful to) and abandoned in the past.

Why did you give up on them? In other words, why were you unfaithful?

Fortunately for us, faithfulness is a fruit of the Holy Spirit and available to us, too, if we will allow the Lord to cultivate it in us. Through the presence of God's Holy Spirit in our hearts, we can grow in faithfulness, but we must walk in close friendship with God. The Bible refers to Him as the One who is called Faithful and True. As we grow to be more like Him, we will become faithful, too.

# Firmly Committed to God's Word

"Papa," she said tearfully, "I *never* want to disobey you. But I must not break the Sabbath. Please, let me read you something suitable, and I'll read this newspaper first thing tomorrow."

Horace gently raised her head from his shoulder and looked into her tear-streaked face. In a tone less harsh but still full of determination, he said: "I had hoped you learned a better lesson from the event of last spring." (Elsie well remembered the terrible day almost a year before, when she had refused to sing a popular song for his guests on the Sabbath.)

"I see now that you think you may do as you like in these matters," Horace continued. "But you are mistaken. I would never ask you to do anything wrong, but I can see no harm in reading that newspaper today. And I am much more capable of judging these matters than you are. Why, I have often seen ministers reading their newspapers on the Sabbath. Surely what is good for them is good enough for you."

Timidly, Elsie responded, "But aren't we supposed to do whatever God tells us without asking what other people do, Papa? Don't very good people sometimes do wrong?"

Growing tired, Horace sank back on his pillow and directed, "Find me a text that says you are not to read a newspaper on Sunday, and I will let you wait until tomorrow."

Elsie thought for some moments. "I can't find one that says just that, Papa," Elsie began slowly, "but the Fourth Commandment says we should keep the Sabbath day holy. In the book of Isaiah, it says we are not to do as we please or go our own way or speak idle words on the Sabbath. Doesn't that mean it is wrong to read worldly thoughts and words on the Sabbath?"

Exasperated, Horace exclaimed, "Nonsense! You are far too young to understand such subjects. Your duty is to obey me. Are you going to read that newspaper?"

Elsie was distraught. She did not want to be disobedient; she wanted always to please her father. But she had a higher duty. "I cannot read it, Papa," she said in a small whisper. "I just can't."

—*Elsie's Impossible Choice*, page 105–106

In the excerpt above, we see how vitally important it was to Elsie to honor God's Word—not out of obligation, but out of steadfast love. Elsie's faithfulness to God, and her desire to be faithful to the commandments in His Word, were unwavering. Even as heart-wrenching as it was for her to be on bad terms with her earthly father and to risk losing his love, she could not and would not betray God.

Have you ever been in a situation where you had to take a strong stand for God or for what you knew in your heart was right, while others around you wanted you to do the opposite? If so, describe it here.

What were the final results of your faithfulness?

Romans 10:17 tells us that "faith comes by hearing the message, and the message is heard through the word of Christ." Unless we know Jesus Christ, we cannot cling to truth. The first step in being faithful is hearing about Jesus and coming to grow in our love and trust for Him. Because the Bible is vital to our relationship with Jesus, it is vital to experiencing the fruit of the Holy Spirit in our lives.

**To live faithfully to our Lord's ways, we must be faithful to His Word.**

As we have discussed, Elsie *loved* God's Word. In fact, above all her wealth, Elsie treasured her little Bible. She turned to it in times of joyful celebration, and in times of trouble. God's Word was often the anchor that held Elsie steady.

How do you feel about the Word of God?

Can you think of a time when the Word of God was like an anchor that held you steady? Describe it here.

By reading our Bibles, we not only learn Scripture, but we also get to know *God's heart*. As your reading and understanding increases, so will your relationship with Him. This wonderful relationship will give you a firm foundation of trust that God will always be there for you. God is a faithful Friend indeed!

# A Note About the Sabbath

As we know, Elsie was firmly committed to the Word of God and tried to be faithful to follow all of the principles she found in it. Because one of the Biblical principles that was very important to Elsie in both *Elsie's Endless Wait* and *Elsie's Impossible Choice* was the principle of honoring the Sabbath, we will mention it here to give you a little more insight on that subject.

Mrs. Murray, the Scottish housekeeper who raised Elsie from birth along with Aunt Chloe, taught Elsie the importance of obeying the Fourth Commandment, which requires the Sabbath day to be kept holy.

Many of the churches of Elsie's day adhered to a set of very strict rules and regulations about what could and could not be done on the Sabbath. Mrs. Murray taught Elsie those rules and she adhered to them steadfastly. As you know, Elsie's determination to obey the Sabbath according to those rules brought her into great conflict with her family and especially with her father.

The establishment of the Sabbath goes all the way back to the book of Genesis. In the second chapter of the book of Genesis, it tells us in verse 3: "God blessed the seventh day and made it holy, because on it he rested from all the work of creating that he had done." Then, in Exodus 16:23, Moses told the Israelites, "This is what the Lord commanded: 'Tomorrow is to be a day of rest, a holy Sabbath to the Lord.'" Isaiah 58:13 instructs us to honor it by not going our own way, not doing as we please, and not speaking idle words.

It is important for you to know that Christians (both today and in Elsie's time) have widely differing views about the Sabbath—about when to celebrate it and what is proper to do and not do on the Sabbath.

Elsie's opinion in *Elsie's Endless Wait* that she could not play the piano on the Sabbath as requested to by her father and her opinion in *Elsie's Impossible Choice* that she could not read the newspaper to him on the Sabbath are views that many people would disagree with today for a number of reasons.

Jesus said in Matthew 12:12 that "it is lawful to *do good* on the Sabbath." Jesus Himself broke the rules that the religious leaders of his day had established when He healed the sick on the Sabbath. In Mark 2:27, Jesus told us, "The Sabbath was made for man, not man for the Sabbath." He referred to Himself as the "Lord of the Sabbath" (Matthew 12:8). And in Matthew 9:13, Jesus said, "I desire mercy, not sacrifice." He made it clear that, in some cases, men had established detailed rules and regulations that were more rigid than God intended and may have even missed the whole point.

Based on the above Scriptures, it can be argued that Jesus might have been pleased if Elsie had, for example, read the newspaper to her sick father. After all, Exodus 20:12, the Fifth Commandment, commanded her to honor her father. Complying with his request would not only have honored him, but been a form of service to an ailing man. In other words, it may have been considered "doing good," which Jesus said in Matthew 12:12 was permitted on the Sabbath.

One thing is clear. God, our Creator, designed the Sabbath as a gift to us. He knows we need one day out of every seven for rest, and He has designated it to meet our needs. He wants the Sabbath to be a delight to us (Isaiah 58:13).

It is very important that you listen carefully to your elders, especially your parents, and to always be teachable on issues such as these—particularly while you are young. Rather than remember Elsie's specific opinions about what she could and couldn't do on the Sabbath, *what is important for us to remember is Elsie's faithful resolve to stand loyal to God and to her Christian conscience, despite the disapproval of others.*

Elsie was completely in love with her Savior. For her, keeping the Sabbath was not an issue of requirements or obligations, but an issue of the heart — one of *pure love for God.* That love was what motivated her to be faithful. God used Elsie's faithfulness to win her father to the Lord, and that illustrates a wonderful principle:

 **When our hearts are faithful to the Lord and we desire to honor Him above everything else, even if we make a mistake — and we will all make mistakes at times — God can and will use the situation for good in our lives.**

That is the promise of Romans 8:28 which says, "And we know that in all things God works for the good of those who love him, who have been called according to his purpose." If we stay humble and teachable, God will always get us back on track! He will honor our efforts to be faithful to Him.

# Faithful in Times of Testing

With his arm around her, Elsie let her head drop upon her father's shoulder. She stood very still, warm in the security of his love that had been absent from her life for such a long time. Never had she been so inclined to make the promise he wanted. With just a few words she could end her banishment. She would no longer face his punishments, no longer dread the possibility that she might be sent away from him forever. With just a few words, she would be enclosed once more in the circle of his love and approval. It would be so easy to restore her father's precious love. But what of the love of Jesus? What of His love which was the most precious of all?

The temptation was great, but it passed quickly, and she spoke in a voice choked with emotion. "There is no one in the world I could ever love as much as I love you, Papa. And I want always to be your obedient daughter. But Jesus tells us that the first and greatest command is to love Him. He says, 'Anyone who loves his father or mother more than me is not worthy of me.' I must love Jesus best and keep His commandments always. Oh, Papa, I can't say I'm sorry that I didn't break His commandment. If you loved Jesus, Papa, you would understand me. I can't choose to obey you and not Him. Please don't ask me to make that choice."

*—Elsie's Impossible Choice,* pages 147–148

*I*n the excerpt above, Elsie quotes Matthew 10:37. When Jesus said this, He was calling us to give first place in our lives and hearts to Him. As much as Elsie loved her precious father—and even after waiting eight long, lonely years for his love—she could not, and would not, choose to be unfaithful to God. When confronted with the pressure to forsake what she saw as God's commandment, Elsie wanted to cry out, *"But there is no choice, Papa! Between God's commands and man's — even yours, Papa — there can never be any choice!"* (see *Elsie's Impossible Choice*, page 111).

 **Elsie models a passion and level of commitment sorely lacking in many of us. How others behaved wasn't the standard that dictated Elsie's choices. For her, there was but one standard— faithfulness to God, even in times of extreme testing.**

In the space below, describe how you tend to respond in times of turmoil and pressure. For example, where do you turn when you are bitterly disappointed, confused, and afraid?

When you have difficulties, what role do you usually allow Jesus to play? (Do you push Him away or do you run into His arms? Do you trust in Him or doubt His strength? Do you remember to involve Him, or do you forget that He exists?) Be honest.

Difficult circumstances can strain any relationship, especially when we don't understand and can't control what's going on. But even then, we must trust Jesus. We need to know and *believe* that He is faithful and that no matter what our circumstances are, He loves us and is at work in our lives.

Aunt Chloe frequently reminded Elsie that God was in the midst of her struggles and would use them for good. Throughout Scripture, we see consistently that our God reigns with sovereign control, using both wonderful things and difficult things to bring about His glory in our lives. Absolutely everything — though we don't always understand why — enters our life by His authority to be used for His good purposes. As we are faithful to trust God in difficult times, our trials push us closer to Him, rather than further apart.

Horace's fury and his promise of more severe punishment terrified Elsie. More than anything he might do, she feared separation and felt that she would surely die if she could not be near her Papa. She could bear his anger and his coldness so long as she could at least see his face and hope that someday his heart would be changed. But what would happen if he sent her away from him? Who else would give her shelter?

It was then that she remembered a verse from Proverbs, and the words calmed her fears and renewed her hope: "The name of the Lord is a strong tower; the righteous run to it and are safe." She imagined a tower of strength that offered refuge from all her earthly trials. Then she reminded herself that Jesus had felt the pain of separation from His Father when He bore the sins of mankind on the Cross. Whatever happened, Elsie knew that Jesus would not forsake her. With these thoughts, she slipped into a peaceful sleep.

—*Elsie's Impossible Choice*, page 149

In the midst of the greatest trial of her life, Elsie envisioned Jesus as a tower of strength offering her shelter and a place to hide from all her earthly troubles! She remembered the verse in Proverbs 18:10 and she knew that the Lord heard her cries. Verse 24 of that same chapter of Proverbs speaks of the Lord, saying, "But there is a friend who sticks closer than a brother." This means that Jesus will stick with us even when others won't—after those closest to us have given up or gone away.

Have you ever experienced a time when you felt Jesus was "closer than a brother" to you? If so, explain.

Through the many circumstances of your life, would you say that you remain faithful and loyal to Jesus no matter what?

Remember, as Proverbs 3:3 encourages us, "Let love and faithfulness *never* leave you; bind them around your neck, write them on the tablet of your heart."

# Faithful in Prayer

> "There's blood on my dress, Papa," Elsie said weakly.
>
> "You fell and hurt your head, but you will be fine now."
>
> "Oh! I remember," she moaned.
>
> Horace helped Chloe, who was steady as a rock even at the sight of so much blood, and they prepared Elsie for bed.
>
> "Are you hungry, darling?" Horace asked.
>
> "No, Papa, I just want to sleep."
>
> So Horace carried her to the bed and was about to tuck her in when Elsie suddenly cried, "My prayers, Papa!"
>
> "Not tonight, dear. You're too weak."
>
> "Please, Papa. I can't sleep otherwise."
>
> So he helped her to her knees and listened as she spoke. To his surprise, he heard his own name mentioned more than once, coupled with a request that he should come to love Jesus.
>
> —*Elsie's Endless Wait*, pages 193–194

As a fruit of the Holy Spirit, being faithful sustains our relationship with God. It keeps us committed to His Word and His ways. Faithfulness causes us to seek His counsel and to desire His presence in all that we do.

If we are living in relationship with our Savior, we will be faithful in prayer. After all, what is friendship but a mutual, two-way relationship. Just as people who love each other desire to talk to each other, our love relationship with God creates a constant and overwhelming need to talk with Him. We do that through prayer. Prayer is conversation with God.

Name three of your closest relationships in the space below. Then answer the following questions: What do you do to communicate with them? How often do you communicate? What are the main ways you maintain your closeness?

Do you realize how easily accessible God is? You do not need an appointment to talk with Him. His line is never busy. His door is always open. He is available to you at *all* times—any time of the day or night. *Through prayer, God is always right there when you want to talk with Him!*

Colossians 4:2 encourages us, "devote yourselves to prayer." First Thessalonians 5:16 urges us to "pray continually." Likewise, Ephesians 6:18 instructs us to "pray in the Spirit on all occasions with all kinds of prayers and requests."

Think about your prayer life and answer the following questions.

1. When do you typically talk with God: mainly in times of need, randomly as He comes to mind, at a set hour each day, or at other times?

2. How do you feel about your conversations with God? (Do you find talking to God automatic and effortless? Do you find it awkward and uncomfortable? Or would you describe it another way?)

3. Do certain things seem easier to pray about than others? If so, give examples.

4. Have you ever experienced comfort and relief from a conversation with Jesus about your difficulties? If so, describe such a time.

5. Do you mostly pray when you want to ask God for something, or do you communicate with Him for other reasons? Explain.

**Prayer is not just about asking God for things. Prayer is sharing your heart with God—telling Him your thoughts, your feelings, and your desires, expressing your fears and concerns, and giving Him your praise.**

To Elsie, Jesus was her most trusted confidant—her very best friend. Though she wasn't privileged with the comfort and companionship of a nurturing family or many friends, Elsie talked to Jesus constantly. Jesus was to her more faithful than even the most loving parent or friend. When we examine her life, we see that Elsie turned to Jesus on most every occasion. Whether she was happy or sad, perfectly content, or had a personal need. Even when she would kneel in tears to pray, always, when Elsie stood again, her hope was restored. Even when Elsie's prayers were not immediately answered—or remained unanswered for years—she did not stop communing with God in prayer. As we read above, Elsie couldn't even go to sleep at night without ending her day talking to God in prayer.

For some people, prayer is an ongoing conversation with a Friend, full of life and energy. To them, it is as simple and yet as vital as breathing. For others, prayer is a duty they must perform like a chore. It is lifeless and boring. Where do you find yourself on the scale between these two extremes? In other words, how do you feel when you pray?

Before you pray next time, ask yourself: "Do I really believe that God is here with me, attentive to my prayers, ready and willing to hear my heart and meet me in my need?" If you cannot respond with a confident "yes," then stop. Put your prayers aside for the moment. Pause, simply to think about God. Contemplate His majesty! Consider that Jesus is alive and well, and His Spirit surrounds you. He is a faithful God. His Word is true; He cannot lie. Foremost, know that His heart overflows with love for you. Think on these things. You might even want to find a promise from His Word that communicates His immense love and power. Let it penetrate your heart. Begin right there by returning to that place of love. Do not let prayer become a lifeless obligation for you. Allow God to show Himself to be real to you again. Never forget His promise that "You will seek me and find me when you seek me with all your heart" (Jeremiah 29:13).

# Faithful to God's Will

"I am very anxious to see this conflict between you and your father resolved. You are both so dear to me, and I cannot bear your unhappiness . . . . Won't you tell me exactly what has happened between the two of you?" said Edward.

In truth, Elsie welcomed this opportunity to share her burden, for Edward Travilla had already proved to be a true and caring friend to her. So she told the story simply: "One Sabbath morning when he was ill — before he became so very ill — he asked me to read him a newspaper that was not fit for the Lord's Day. I couldn't do it, Mr. Travilla. I couldn't go against God's commandment to keep the Sabbath day holy. But Papa says I must apologize for not obeying him. And I must promise *never* to disobey him in the future. Until I promise, I am banished from his affection. But I can't do what Papa asks. No matter how much I love my Papa, I can't choose him over God."

There was no defiance in her voice. Edward heard only sorrow in Elsie's words and tone, so he knew that this was not a matter of childish willfulness.

"But if reading that newspaper to your father really were a sin," he said soothingly, "surely it would be a very little one. I can't believe that God would be angry with you for such a small thing."

"But, Mr. Travilla," Elsie replied, "if only you knew how much I *want* to obey Papa. But my conscience tells me it is wrong!"

—*Elsie's Impossible Choice*, page 135

As we discussed earlier, faithfulness is what gives us staying power in relationships. Those of us who have enjoyed close relationships know that being faithful to a friend requires work—with much give and take. We can't always do what we want. Oftentimes, simply for the sake of our friend, we engage in activities that hold little or no appeal other than the fact that she enjoys them. Unless we're willing to appreciate her interests, we don't make a very good friend.

Just as we need to work to maintain a close relationship with our friend, so also we need to "work" to maintain a close relationship with God. One of the ways we do that is by doing the things that are important to Him, and those things are described in His

Word. That is another reason why we obey His commands. Obedience shows Him how much we love Him. It shows that we care about the things that matter to God.

*God loves you so much that He cares about the details of your life. He wants to give you guidance, for that is one of the ways He expresses to you His love.* Yet have you ever thought about the fact that every day of our lives, we routinely make choices without even wondering, let alone asking, what God thinks about it. Instead, we "do our own thing."

When making plans with others, how often do you consider what God wants you to do?

For each of the following categories, list some examples of the ways we take it upon ourselves to "do our own thing" without involving God.

With friends:

With activities:

With our possessions and money:

Earlier in this study guide in the section on kindness, we discussed the concept of our "center" and talked about how for most people, the bulk of their time and attention is invested in themselves. We learned that kindness requires us to be other-centered. Faithfulness has a similar requirement. In order to be faithful to someone else, we must often take our attention off of ourselves.

**If we desire to live a life that is faithful to God, we must center our lives on Him.**

A person who centers her life around herself and her own interests and feelings is a "self-centered" person. Most of us can think of someone who is self-centered to an extreme, and we usually do not want to be around that person. Enna Dinsmore is a good example.

When we live a "God-centered" life, we think about what God would want over anything else. We center our attention on Him. This means that we seek to live our lives in ways that will please and honor Him.

In the chart below are listed some of the attributes of a self-centered life. Rewrite those attributes by changing them instead to their opposite, God-centered counterparts. You can also add others to the list.

| SELF-CENTERED LIFE | GOD-CENTERED LIFE |
| --- | --- |
| independent, self-reliant | dependent on God |
| selfish | giving and willing to share |
| mean | kind |
| anxious and worried | |
| bragging about ourselves | |
| judgmental of others | |
| prideful | |
| disobedient | |
| dishonest | |
| insensitive to others' feelings | |
| impatient | |
| | |

**The Bible teaches us that our lives are not intended to be about ourselves and our agendas, but about God and *His* agenda! If we want to be faithful to God, we need to be faithful to become like Him, for this is His desire for us — to form the character of Jesus in us.**

Do you know that God made each of us for His specific purposes? As we read in the previous chapter on goodness, "For we are God's workmanship, created in Christ Jesus to do good works, which God prepared in advance for us to do" (Ephesians 2:10).

Have you ever wondered what purposes God holds for your life? Have you ever greeted the day asking the Holy Spirit to direct your steps and empower you to perform His will for your life that day? The seasons of your life are periods of training and instruction for the destiny God has in store for you.

We see in the apostle Paul's life that he sought God's will regularly, even in his daily tasks. Paul declared, "But I will come to you very soon, *if the Lord is willing*" (1 Corinthians 4:19). "I will come back *if it is God's will*" (Acts 18:21). "I hope to spend some time with you, *if the Lord permits*" (1 Corinthians 16:7). "And *God permitting*, we will do so" (Hebrews 6:3). If we are to live God-centered lives, like Paul, we need to let God lead us each step of the way.

Can you think of any dangers of neglecting to seek God's direction in our life?

Perhaps the Holy Spirit is nudging you at this very moment to pray to God about the direction for your life. Pause and invite Him to speak to you. Ask Him for the fruit of faithfulness to grow in you so that you will be faithful to do God's will. Ask Him to help you remember that He should be first in your life. If you should feel led, rededicate your life to Him right now. Write your thoughts or prayers in the space below.

Look back over this chapter. Ask the Holy Spirit to show you the most important things He wants you to remember. Put a star beside those truths and, in your own words, summarize below what He showed you.

Rewrite your thoughts as a prayer, asking God to help you grow and apply the truths He's taught you throughout the chapter.

Write out the memory verse for this chapter:

Write out Galatians 5:22–23, the memory verse for our entire study guide:

# CHAPTER

8

# *Walking in Gentleness*

# Walking In Gentleness

Your beauty should not come from outward adornment, such as braided hair and the wearing of gold jewelry and fine clothes. Instead, it should be that of your inner self, the unfading beauty of a gentle and quiet spirit, which is of great worth in God's sight.

— 1 PETER 3:3–4

## Gentle in Heart

Elsie had learned how to yield readily to others, and when she experienced some unjust or unkind treatment, she would go to her Bible. Her communings with her beloved Savior made everything right again, and she would emerge as serenely happy as if nothing had happened. Her attitude bewildered the family. Her grandfather would sometimes contemplate her behavior when she graciously gave up her wishes to Enna. Then he'd shake his head and say to himself, "That girl's no Dinsmore, or she'd stand up for her rights better than that. She can't be Horace's child, for it never was easy to impose on him. He was a boy of spirit, not like this child."

Even Adelaide had remarked to Rose that Elsie was a "strange" child. "I'm often surprised to see how sweetly she gives in to all of us," Adelaide observed. "Really, she has a lovely temperament. I envy her, for it was always hard for me to give up my own way or forgive those who teased me."

"I don't think it has been easy for Elsie either," Rose said. "But the Bible tells us that it is to a person's glory to overlook an offense. I think her sweet disposition is the fruit of a work of grace in her heart. It is 'the unfading beauty of a gentle and quiet spirit' which God alone can bestow."

"I wish I had that," Adelaide sighed.

"You only have to go to the right source, dear Adelaide," Rose replied kindly.

"And yet," Adelaide went on, "I must say that sometimes I think, as Papa says, that there is something mean-spirited and cowardly in always giving up to others."

"It would be cowardly and wrong to give up *principle*," Rose said, "but surely it is noble and generous to give up our own wishes to another, when no principle is involved."

"Of course, you're right," Adelaide mused. "And now that I think of it, although Elsie gives in on her wishes readily enough, I've never known her to sacrifice principle. On the contrary, she has made Mamma very angry several times by refusing to play with Enna on the Sabbath or to lie to Papa about Arthur's misdeeds. Elsie is certainly very different from the rest of us, and if it's godliness that makes her what she is, then I think godliness is a lovely thing."

—*Elsie's Endless Wait*, pages 36–37

*A*s we have seen in the previous chapters, Elsie walked in the fruit of the Holy Spirit—and other people noticed! Her behavior was always puzzling to the people around her. Even her aunt Adelaide called Elsie a "strange child." There is no doubt about it: without ever intending to draw attention to herself, Elsie caught people's attention.

Now we will look at Elsie's gentleness. In your own words, describe what you think "gentleness" means.

Not only can you be gentle with objects or things (like gently holding a baby chick), but you can also be gentle in the way you express yourself with others. What do you think being gentle in the way you express yourself to others would mean? (Be specific.)

What do you think of gentleness? Do you desire to become more gentle yourself? Does gentleness in yourself or other people bother you because it seems too soft, or do you admire it?

List any specific areas in your life where you want to become more gentle.

How did we see the virtue of gentleness displayed in Elsie's life? Give some examples.

How did most of the Dinsmores regard Elsie's gentle disposition?

Like the Dinsmores, sometimes we, too, view a gentle spirit as weak and insignificant, lacking the ability to assert oneself. But gentleness is anything but weak or shy.

Consider what Jesus says about Himself in Matthew 11:28–30. He says, "Come to me, all you who are weary and burdened, and I will give you rest. Take my yoke upon you and learn from me, *for I am gentle* and humble in heart, and you will find rest for your souls. For my yoke is easy and my burden is light."

Yet, as gentle as Jesus was, read this description about Him from Revelations 1:14–16. It says, "His eyes were like blazing fire. His feet were like bronze glowing in a furnace, and his voice was like the sound of rushing waters. In his right hand he held seven stars, and out of his mouth came a sharp double-edged sword. His face was like the sun shining in all its brilliance." Yes, the gentle Lamb of God is also the Lion of Judah.

 **Make no mistake. Gentleness *does not* mean weakness.**

Before we discuss more about the strength of gentleness, look up the following Scriptures in your Bible. Write them out and think about the pictures they give us of gentleness.

Zechariah 9:9 –

1 Thessalonians 2:6–7 –

Jesus riding on a donkey . . . like a mother caring for her children. Just reading about these images almost makes us sit back and relax. There is something soothing about gentleness, for gentleness is calm, mild, and soft, not severe, harsh, or rough. Gentleness is a lamblikeness — or dove-likeness — often translated in Scripture as meekness or humility.

This marvelous virtue can be ours as we bow our hearts before God. Through the fruit of gentleness birthed in us by the power of the Holy Spirit, we submit ourselves to our Lord and Savior — our Lamb and our Lion — Jesus Christ. With His help, we can do what the apostle Paul instructed us to do: "Let your gentleness be evident to all" (Philippians 4:5).

Pause now and pray for the Lord to help you grow in the fruit of gentleness.

# Unfading Beauty

But what, indeed, did the father expect of his daughter? Horace Dinsmore, Jr. was, like his father, an upright and moral man who paid outward respect to the forms of religion but cared nothing for the vital power of godliness. Horace trusted his own morality entirely, and he regarded most Christians as hypocrites and deceivers. He had been told of his little Elsie's Christian devotion, and though he didn't acknowledge it even to himself, this information had prejudiced him against his child.

—*Elsie's Endless Wait*, page 51

In our last section, we learned about being gentle in heart. Now we will look at one of the opposites of gentleness: pride. You could say that pride opposes gentleness. Unlike "a gentle and quiet spirit," pride creates a restless, anxious stirring within us that causes us to become harsh, rude, impatient, and unyielding. Unsatisfied with who we are, we attempt to build ourselves up by tearing others down. This is what Horace was doing in the passage above.

Look in the mirror. What do you see? Two eyes looking back at you? A nice hairstyle . . . a "funny-looking" nose (according to you, maybe, but certainly not to your mother!) . . . a pretty smile . . . crooked teeth . . . freckles . . . dimples? Or when you look in the mirror, do you see a person — someone that you like? A person with unique talents . . . a person who loves Jesus . . . a person who has a bright future ahead of her? Do you see someone special, beloved by God — the very apple of His eye?

There are times when we look in the mirror and lose sleep from focusing intently on something as small as a pimple! We fret constantly over our appearance because we think it determines who we are.

When the Lord looks at you, what do you think His biggest concerns are?

In 1 Peter 3:3–4, our memory verse, the apostle Peter addresses our obsession with outward appearances. Write out that verse below.

By this verse, Peter is not condemning time invested in our appearances. He is simply telling us the definition of *true* beauty.

What do you think the phrase "a gentle and quiet spirit" means?

 **If a gentle and quiet spirit is something that is of great worth in God's sight, then it is something that we want to have!**

Look up the definition of the word "unfading" in your dictionary. Write the definition of it here.

 **True beauty—inner beauty—does not get wrinkles! It does not need makeup to make it look good and it does not diminish over time! That is why it is so important to let the Holy Spirit form that kind of beauty inside of us.**

Unfortunately, however, most of us spend our time examining how we look on the outside and closely analyzing the outward appearance of others. As if we were beauty pageant judges, we critique other people's looks, personalities, behaviors, etc.—not just our own.

Why do you think we get so distracted by trivial matters like *outward* appearance while we ignore the things that are important to God?

One of the answers is pride. Pride plagues our human nature. It's who we are apart from God — self-centered, self-focused, snobbish and critical towards others. Pride leads us directly to sin.

Pride was, in fact, the very first sin. It is what led Satan to fall from Heaven—he wanted to be equal to God. And it is what led Adam and Eve into sin—they wanted to become like God by eating the forbidden fruit.

Our Lord explains in Matthew 23:12, "For whoever exalts himself will be humbled, and whoever humbles himself will be exalted." In Psalm 18:27, David proclaims, "You save the humble but bring low those whose eyes are haughty." Scripture tells us plainly, "God opposes the proud but gives grace to the humble" (see James 4:6).

In what way are you being proud when you are critical of how people look?

# Yielding to Others

At last Adelaide spoke again. "Elsie is an odd child, and I don't really understand her. She is so meek and patient that she will virtually allow the other children to trample her. Her meekness provokes my Papa, and he says she is no Dinsmore because she doesn't know how to stand up for herself. Yet Elsie does have a temper, I know. Ever so often it shows itself, but just for an instant. Then she grieves over it as if she had committed some crime, whereas the rest of us think nothing of getting angry a dozen times a day.

— *Elsie's Endless Wait, page 19*

Gentleness, as a fruit of the Holy Spirit, causes us to be willing to yield to others. Although, as we discussed, people might mistakenly look at this as a sign of weakness, in reality, this kind of gentleness requires a true strength of character. It involves deferring to another's judgment, authority, opinion, or interests *by choice*. To "yield" or "defer" to others means to desire or allow that anothers' needs are met *before your own*. For instance, instead of squabbling over what video to watch, you agree to watch the one that your brother or sister desires to see. For many of us, this is very hard.

**If we are to have the fruit of gentleness, we must learn to humbly give up our own rights, not due to lack of courage, but because we intentionally choose to surrender to the will of God—just as Jesus submitted to the will of the Father.**

It is not always easy to submit to the will of the Lord. Pride rises up within us and causes us to want our own will and desires. Pride bows to no one, whereas gentleness, or meekness, readily submits to God and is willing to yield to others. Pride makes us hard and unyielding; gentleness makes us as soft and tame as a lamb or a dove.

When we freely give up our rights to people they will often misunderstand us. In Elsie's case, her grandfather thought she was "no Dinsmore" because she did not seem to know how to stand up for herself.

How do you typically "stand up for yourself?" When you do not get what you want, what is your usual reaction?

Can you remember a time where you got in an argument because you wanted something that someone else did not? Describe it here.

Remember the discussion of Rose and Adelaide that began this chapter? In it Adelaide had commented on how graciously and sweetly Elsie gave up her wishes to Enna and the other members of the family when no *principle* was involved. Why is the distinction between a wish and a principle important?

Do you find it hard to give up your wishes to others? Why or why not?

Do you have trouble yielding your desires to some people, but not to others? Explain.

When we are stubborn, bossy, rebellious, demanding, etc., are we walking in the fruit of the Spirit?

When we find that we have acted in those ways, what would the Lord want us to do?

# Persecuted for His Name's Sake

"What's all this fuss?" he roared.

"Nothing," said his wife, whose voice had suddenly grown sweet, "except that Enna is not well enough to go out and wants a fairy tale to help pass the time. And your granddaughter" — she stared pointedly at Elsie — "is too lazy or willful to tell it."

Mr. Dinsmore turned on Elsie. "Is that so? Well, there's an old saying, little girl. 'A bird that *can* sing and *won't* sing must be *made* to sing.'"

Elsie, who knew the meaning of the saying all too well, started to speak, but Mrs. Dinsmore cut her off. "The child pretends it is all on account of conscientious scruples. She says it isn't fit for the Sabbath. I don't care what that Mrs. Murray taught her. *I* say it is a great impertinence for a child of Elsie's age to set her opinion against yours and mine. I know very well it's just an excuse because she doesn't choose to oblige."

"Of course, it's an excuse," Mr. Dinsmore said hotly. Though by nature a just man, he also had a quick and often unreasonable temper, like all the Dinsmores.

Elsie spoke up, "No, Grandpa. It's not an excuse — "

"How dare you contradict me, you impudent little girl!" Catching her by the arm, he set her down hard on a chair. "Now, little miss," he shouted, "don't move from that chair till your father comes home. Then we'll see what he thinks of such impertinence. If he doesn't give you the punishment you deserve, I miss my guess."

"Please, Grandpa, I — "

Again he stopped her. "Hold your tongue, girl!" he bellowed. "And not another word until your father comes."

*—Elsie's Endless Wait*, pages 174–175

In his famous teaching to his followers called the Sermon on the Mount, Jesus declared, "Blessed are those who are persecuted because of righteousness, for theirs is the kingdom of heaven" (Matthew 5:10). Just as Jesus was persecuted for doing what was right, Elsie was often persecuted for doing what she felt was right in the eyes of God. What Matthew 5:10 promises us is that even though persecution for doing right is a difficult thing to bear, our reward will be great because of it!

Jesus went on to say, "Blessed are you when men hate you, when they exclude you and insult you and reject your name as evil, because of the Son of Man. Rejoice in that day and leap for joy, *because great is your reward in heaven*. For that is how their fathers treated the prophets" (Luke 6:22–23).

Rejoice, indeed! If persecution measures how closely we resemble our Lord, then persecution carries great honor. If you are being persecuted for your righteousness, this is a good sign. It means that you are walking closer to Jesus and becoming more like Him!

What do you think the rewards in Heaven might be for someone who has been persecuted because of righteousness? Make a list.

Has persecution ever caused you to regret obedience to Jesus?

Have you ever regretted being disobedient to Jesus? If so, give an example.

When we tend to please everyone, when we're popular in all circles and mix well with this world, chances are we're not standing up for God. Jesus said, "If the world hates you, keep in mind that it hated me first. If you belonged to the world, it would love you as its own. As it is, you do not belong to the world, but I have chosen you out of the world. That is why the world hates you" (John 15:18–19).

Time and again, we saw how Elsie was mistreated because of her Christian beliefs. Have you ever been treated poorly because of your faith in Jesus? If so, were you able to maintain gentleness in the face of it?

Consider these verses: "A gentle answer turns away wrath, but a harsh word stirs up anger" (Proverbs 15:1), and "Through patience a ruler can be persuaded, and a gentle tongue can break a bone" (Proverbs 25:15). What do those verses tell us about the *power* of gentleness?

# Spending Your Inheritance

"But Elsie [asked Lora], can you tell me how to be a true Christian? I want to try very hard and never rest until I am one."

Elsie was overjoyed, and she picked up her little Bible. "Let me show you Jesus' words," she said, finding the verse she wanted. "'For everyone who asks, receives; he who seeks, finds; and to him who knocks, the door will be opened.' That must encourage you.

"And see this verse: 'You will seek me and find me when you seek me with all your heart.' Oh, dear Lora, all you have to do is seek Him. The Bible promises that if you seek the Lord with all your heart, you will find Him."

"Yes," Lora said a little doubtfully, "but how do I seek Him, and what must I do to be saved?"

Elsie, who knew the Bible more thoroughly than most children her age, recalled the answer that Paul the apostle gave to the jailer: "'Believe in the Lord Jesus Christ, and you will be saved.'" She turned to the tenth chapter of the book of Romans and read aloud: "If you confess with your mouth, 'Jesus is Lord,' and believe in your heart that God raised Him from the dead, you will be saved.'

"You see, Lora," said Elsie, "you simply have to believe in Jesus. But you must believe with your heart — not just your mind."

"But how do I get rid of my sins? How do I make myself pleasing in the sight of God?" Lora asked eagerly.

Elsie turned to the book of First John. "See what it says here, Lora?" she asked. "'The blood of Jesus Christ, His Son, purifies us from all sin.' Jesus has already done all that is necessary. We have nothing to do but to believe in Him and accept His offer of forgiveness of sins and eternal life. Just accept them as free gifts, and then love and trust Him."

"But surely I must *do* something?" Lora asked.

Elsie thought carefully. "Well," she replied, "God says, 'Give me your heart.' You can do that. You can invite Him to come live in your heart. You can tell Him how much you need Him. And the Bible says, 'If we confess our sins, He is faithful and just and will forgive us our sins and purify us from all unrighteousness.' So you can tell Jesus your sins and ask Him to forgive them. You can ask Him to teach you to be sorry for your sins and give you a desire to be like Him — loving and kind and forgiving. Of course, we can't be like Him without the help of His Holy Spirit. But we can always get that help if we ask.

"Oh, Lora, don't be afraid to ask. Don't be afraid to come to Jesus. But you must come humbly, for the Bible says 'God opposes the proud, but gives grace to the humble.' He won't turn away anyone who comes to Him humbly, seeking to be saved."

For the rest of the afternoon, Lora stayed with Elsie, asking questions and reading from the Scriptures. Elsie explained that being a Christian meant having Jesus in your heart, not just attending church and reading the Bible. Then they sang a hymn together, and Elsie talked about her own peace and joy in believing in Jesus. "Oh, how good of God to make being saved so easy that anyone can do it — even children like us," she exclaimed.

*—Elsie's Endless Wait*, pages 128–130

We named this section "Spending Your Inheritance" because that is what the Lord asks of us. When we accept Jesus as Lord of our lives, our inheritance is the forgiveness of sins and eternal life. By telling others about Jesus and helping them come to know Him, you are giving them a wonderful gift. They too will have an inheritance. This is God's plan, that we would spread the good news!

Do you have a heart for the lost? Do you pray for those who don't know Jesus? Do you live in such a way that others will see the love and power of Jesus Christ in your life? These are questions that every Christian should ask him or herself.

As those filled with the Holy Spirit of God Himself, we should have our hearts and minds set on these things and desire to see others come into the kingdom of God. This heart was wonderfully magnified in the life of Elsie.

List ways that you can recall which demonstrate how Elsie loved the lost and expressed her love for Jesus to them.

What are some ways that we can draw others to Jesus? Be specific.

Whether Elsie was praying for people, submitting to God and those around her, discussing her love relationship with Jesus, or simply "being Elsie," her life constantly pointed others to the Lord. *Elsie had the wonderful ability to make people want to know more about Jesus.* Many people left her presence wanting that mysterious "something" that she seemed to possess. Often, it was Elsie's gentleness that spoke louder than words!

Have you ever heard of non-Christians complaining that Christians "beat them over the head with the Bible?" This is a figurative expression that means they feel that Christians are too pushy or harsh with them.

Can you think of some ways in which a "gentle and quiet spirit" could help draw such people to Jesus?

First Peter 3:15 says, "But in your hearts set apart Christ as Lord. Always be prepared to give an answer to everyone who asks you to give the reason for the hope that you have. But do this with *gentleness* and respect. . . ."

 **Gentleness opens the door of people's hearts and has the power to win the lost.**

List some unsaved people you know in your life. Take some time to pray for them now.

Look back over this chapter. Ask the Holy Spirit to show you the most important things He wants you to remember. Put a star beside those truths and, in your own words, summarize below what He showed you.

Rewrite your thoughts as a prayer, asking God to help you grow and apply the truths He's taught you throughout the chapter.

Write out the memory verse for this chapter:

Write out Galatians 5:22–23, the memory verse for our entire study guide:

# CHAPTER

**9**

## Walking in Self-Control

### Lesson 1
*The Spirit-Controlled Life*

### Lesson 2
*Choose This Day Whom You Will Serve*

### Lesson 3
*Taming Our Emotions*

### Lesson 4
*All Things Unto God*

### Lesson 5
*Against Such Things
There Is No Law*

# Walking In Self-Control

For God did not give us a spirit of timidity, but a spirit of power, of love and of self-discipline.

—2 Timothy 1:7

## The Spirit-Controlled Life

"Why don't you speak?" Miss Day demanded, and she grabbed Elsie by the arm and shook the girl roughly. "Answer me this instant! Why have you been idling all morning, you lazy girl?"

"I haven't been idling," Elsie protested quickly. "I tried hard to do my work, and you're punishing me when I don't deserve it."

"How dare you? There!" Miss Day shouted, smacking Elsie hard on the ear. "Take that for your impertinence!"

Elsie wanted to shout her own harsh reply, but she restrained herself. Looking at her book, she tried to study, but her ear ached painfully and hot tears came so fast that she could not see the page.

—*Elsie's Endless Wait*, page 11

At last, you have made it to the very last chapter of *Elsie's Life Lessons: Walking in the Fruit of the Spirit!* Fantastic work! You are on the home stretch!

Now we tackle the last, but not least, dimension of the fruit of the Holy Spirit—self-control.

Self-control is an instrument of government — self-government. It's the means of keeping ourselves under control, within proper and healthy boundaries. Exercising self-control means having power over one's self. In other words, it means controlling, curbing, or restraining one's desires, emotions or actions. Simply put, self-control *chooses to restrain itself* out of love and respect for God and others.

Look up the word "restrain" in your dictionary and write the definition here.

Most of us recognize the acronym *W.W.J.D. – What Would Jesus Do?* This question continuously enters the minds and hearts of those who live a Spirit-controlled life — a life where we let the Spirit of God guide and control our actions instead of just taking action ourselves. In every thought, decision, and response, the desire to seek Jesus and follow His ways overrides all other desires.

This is what we saw in Elsie's life. As we read the *A Life of Faith: Elsie Dinsmore* series, this example is constantly held up before us. Elsie did not live according to rules and regulations. She was not dominated by a list of *dos* and *don'ts* or by mere obligations. On the contrary, Elsie loved God with all of her heart, and her life reflected that love.

In the previous excerpt, Elsie wanted to shout back at Miss Day when she was unfairly accused. But she *restrained herself.* Had she just been relying on her *own ability* to hold back her outrage, she would not have been able to do it. But Elsie relied on the power of the *Holy Spirit* within her. As our memory verse tells us, "For God did not give us a spirit of timidity, but a spirit of power, of love, and of *self-discipline*" (2 Timothy 1:7). Self-discipline is another word for self-control.

Wait! Did you see that? Read the passage again. God has *already given you* a spirit of self-discipline! You have the ability. Now you just need to learn how to tap into it!

 **We can rely on God's Spirit within us to help us restrain ourselves.**

Read the following verses and think about what they mean in regard to self-control:

❖ "Like a city whose walls are broken down is a man who lacks self-control" (Proverbs 25:28).

❖ "A fool gives full vent to his anger, but a wise man keeps himself under control" (Proverbs 29:11).

❖ "A man of knowledge uses words with restraint, and a man of understanding is even-tempered" (Proverbs 17:27).

❖ "Even a fool is thought wise if he keeps silent, and discerning if he holds his tongue" (Proverbs 17:28).

What conclusions can be drawn about self-control from those verses?

When Elsie withheld her anger at Miss Day, it was as an act of self-control. What other ways can someone show self-control? List them here.

Can you think of an instance this past week where you should have exhibited self-control and didn't? What happened?

In what area do you think you *most* lack self-control?

List some areas where you would like to have more self-control.

Our Lord tells us, "I will instruct you and teach you in the way you should go; I will counsel you and watch over you. Do not be like the horse or the mule, which have no understanding but must be controlled by bit and bridle or they will not come to you" (Psalm 32:8–9). Our heavenly Father desires to give us, with the help of His Holy Spirit, the unseen bridle of His love through the fruit of self-control.

# Choose This Day Whom You Will Serve

"Miss Day," Lora said indignantly, "since Arthur won't speak up, I have to tell you that it's all his fault that Elsie failed her lessons. She tried her very best, but he was teasing her constantly, and he also made her spill the ink on her copybook. She was too honorable to tear out the page or let him do her arithmetic, which he said he would do."

"Is this so, Arthur?" Miss Day demanded angrily.

The boy hung his head but didn't reply.

"Alright then," Miss Day said, "you will stay at home as well."

Lora was amazed. "Surely you won't punish Elsie now that I've told you it wasn't her fault."

Miss Day only turned her haughty gaze on Lora, and with ice in her voice, she said, "Understand this, Miss Lora. I will not be dictated to by any of my pupils."

Lora bit her lip, but she said nothing more.

As the other children recited their lessons, Elsie sat at her desk and struggled with the feelings of anger and indignation that were boiling inside her. Although she possessed a gentle and quiet spirit, Elsie was not perfect, and she often had to do fierce battle with her naturally quick temper. But because she seldom displayed her anger to others, it was commonly said within the family that Elsie had no spirit.

*—Elsie's Endless Wait*, pages 8–9

If we live a lifestyle of self-control, people will not always understand us. As we saw in the previous chapter on the fruit of gentleness, to those in her family, Elsie was seen as having "no spirit." But in reality, she was full of spirit—the Holy Spirit! She simply sought, through the power of the Holy Spirit, to manage her emotions. That same strength is available to you. For God did not give YOU a spirit of timidity, but a spirit of power, of love and of self-discipline (2 Timothy 1:7)!

Jesus said, "No one can serve two masters" (Matthew 6:24). Here is a question for you: How many masters are you trying to serve?

*What?* you ask with eyebrows raised. *Masters? I don't have any of those in my life!* But don't be too hasty to answer. This word is foreign to us apart from our reference to Jesus and biblical times. Just because we don't relate to the terms used two thousand years ago, however, doesn't mean that numerous little "masters" don't fight for authority over us all the time.

A "master" is anything that possesses power to rule over us. It's anything — a person, place, occupation, hobby, goal, desire, or possession — that causes us to act a certain way. Both good and bad things can become masters that seize control of our hearts and minds.

List ten things that young people commonly experience as masters.

If you listed friends, peer pressure, money, wanting to belong and fit in with others, you're well on your way to understanding and identifying modern-day masters.

How does a master compete with God in our lives?

Behind many masters lurks a culprit: Fear—fear of rejection, fear of failure, fear of being left out, and so on. Fear causes us to feel and behave contrary to or opposite from the will and the ways of God.

There's only one good type of fear. We're told in Deuteronomy 6:13, "Fear the Lord your God and serve him only. . . ."

What do you think it means to "fear" God?

Sometimes we misunderstand what it means to fear the Lord. Because worldly fear is a negative emotion that anticipates harm, we might think that to fear the Lord indicates that God is a tyrant or bully of some kind. Of course nothing could be further from the truth. From our studies in *Elsie's Life Lessons* we know that God is gracious and kind and full of love for us.

**To "fear the Lord" means to show Him great honor and reverence. It includes a deep sense of love, respect and awe.**

When we "fear God," we desire to honor God first and we live to love and please Him. Worldly threats and concerns fade away. To fear God is a wonderful thing because it sets our minds on things above. As we turn our every concern toward our beautiful Savior, worldly fears lose their grip on us.

Remember what our Lord taught in Matthew 6:24—we cannot serve two masters. This is why Paul says, "If I were still trying to please men, I would not be a servant of Christ" (Galatians 1:10). You see, we can't please men and be able to please God at the same time. Trying to please others is called a "fear of man."

In your own words, describe how a "fear of man" would interfere with living for Jesus and following His ways.

When we fear the thoughts and opinions of others, what are some of the ways we behave?

Describe a circumstance when the "fear of man" caused you to behave in a manner opposite what you knew to be godly and right.

Our heavenly Father assures us that there is no need to fear others. God is far more powerful than any man. He does not want us to be afraid of the opinions or even insults of other people. He wants us to keep our eyes fixed on Him!

Have you ever experienced a time when your love for God helped you to overcome your fears of other people? Explain it here.

With a desire to obey Jesus, sadly, Elsie occasionally offended her father. But in the end, her love for the Lord won her father's heart. Her fear of God—her reverence for Him above all—caused Horace to look at God, thus allowing his eyes to eventually be opened to the fact that Jesus was, in fact, the Savior of all.

# Taming Our Emotions

"Won't your father let you eat *anything* good?" asked Mary Leslie. "Is he cross with you?"

Before Elsie could answer, Lucy piped up, "Elsie's father is so hard on her. When I was here last summer, he never let her have anything sweet or tasty. He makes her drink milk instead of coffee and eat cold breads instead of hot, and she can't even have a bit of butter. I do think he is the *strictest* man I ever saw."

Elsie's face had turned a bright red as anger rose inside her. "That's not true, Lucy," she said with intense feeling. "My Papa only does what is best for me. And I can eat almost anything I want."

"He is quite correct, too," said Mrs. Brown. "Elsie's father takes excellent care of her, and I have noticed that she is much stronger and healthier since Mr. Dinsmore's return." Then the good housekeeper looked pointedly at Lucy Carrington. "You know that too much rich food and too many late hours can be very harmful to growing children."

Lucy blushed and looked down at her own plate, which she had piled high with muffins and creamy cakes.

"I think that Elsie's father loves her very dearly," said Carrie Howard soothingly. To Elsie, she added, "Anyone can see that just by the way he looks at you."

Carrie then proceeded to change the subject, and the girls were soon planning the rest of their day and laughing as usual. But Elsie did not wholly forget her angry feelings. Though some people said she was too meek for her own good, Elsie had a quick temper and often had to struggle to control it. She was truly grateful to Carrie and Mrs. Brown for their kind defense of her father.

—*Elsie's Impossible Choice*, pages 29–30

Like Elsie, we all encounter regretful emotions such as jealousy, envy, discord, and rage. But the apostle Paul reminds us of the grace available to us in Jesus. He says, "live by the Spirit, and you will not gratify the desires of the sinful nature" (Galatians 5:16). We saw this in Elsie's example. Though just a young child, she was able to conquer difficult emotions and walk in godliness. How did she do it? By the power of the Holy Spirit, of course. Through the fruit of self-control, Elsie turned away from her anger and turned toward Jesus. If Elsie had lost her temper and spoken out of anger, we can all agree that she would have regretted it terribly. But Elsie walked in self-control!

In *Elsie's Endless Wait*, we read:

> Despite her youth, Elsie was beginning to learn how to control her own emotions, and in a few moments, she had recovered her composure so that she could return to the breakfast room and take her place at the table. Her sweet face was sad indeed and showed the traces of tears, but it was also calm and peaceful.
> —*Elsie's Endless Wait*, page 57

Self-control does not mean that we never cry or acknowledge the hurt and pain in a situation. There will be occasions when our hurt overwhelms us and we do break down in tears. But notice how self-control helped Elsie *regain* her composure.

 **If we let it, self-control will be at work before, during, and after the wave of emotion crashes upon us. Even when we lose control of our emotions, self-control can help us gain it back.**

Do you know what "composure" means? Look up this word in a dictionary or ask a parent or friend to explain it. Write the meaning below.

How can we regain our composure when we have lost it?

Look up the following verses in your Bible and write them out below. After each one, describe in your own words what the verse suggests to us about self-control.

Proverbs 14:16 –

James 1:19 –

Colossians 3:2 –

Emotions can cause us to say and do things we may later regret. Through the fruit of self-control, however, God equips us to tame our emotions.

The apostle Peter writes, "Finally, all of you, live in harmony with one another; be sympathetic, love as brothers, be compassionate and humble. Do not repay evil with evil or insult with insult, but with blessing, because to this you were called so that you may inherit a blessing. For, 'Whoever would love life and see good days must keep his tongue from evil and his lips from deceitful speech. He must turn from evil and do good; he must seek peace and pursue it'" (1 Peter 3:8–11).

To exercise self-control when it comes to our emotions, our actions, and our words is not always easy. To help us do it, what kind of spirit has God given us, according to 2 Timothy 1:7, our memory verse?

Pause now to pray and ask the Lord to help you grow in the fruit of self-control. Let Him know you are willing to change and that you want Him to help you.

# All Things Unto God

And Elsie did work to obey her father's command. Even when she was alone, she struggled mightily to restrain her feelings and her tears. She was not always successful, but as she battled with her immense sorrow, she sought answers to her difficulties. She remembered these words from the book of Psalms: "God is our refuge and strength, an ever-present help in trouble." And she turned more and more to her Bible and her Heavenly Friend. Deprived of Horace's company, Elsie spent her time with God and His Word, and there she found "the peace that transcends all understanding." With the peace of God in her heart, her ability to meet the trials of each day was renewed and strengthened.

— _Elsie's Impossible Choice_, page 127

As can be seen in the above passage, no matter what the circumstances, Elsie kept her heart and mind focused on the Lord. The Lord was her first priority and her refuge and strength. Her heavenly Friend was who she most wanted to please.

If we were honest with ourselves, we would have to say that we live to please ourselves or other people more than God. But God's Word gives us this instruction: "Whatever you do, work at it with all your heart, _as working for the Lord_, not for men . . ." (Colossians 3:23).

When we approach our schoolwork, it seems reasonable to have our teachers in mind. And when we tackle our household responsibilities, it seems wise to consider our parents. To do all things as Colossians 3 suggests, "with all our hearts, as working for the Lord," seems like an enormous undertaking. In truth, however, learning to do all things as unto God brings great relief in our everyday lives.

What do you think it means to work _for the Lord?_

In your daily tasks, how do you go about working "for the Lord?"

How do you think our work is affected if we do it with a heart to please God? Give some examples.

It is not wrong to want to please significant people in your life, such as your parents, teachers, youth leaders, or friends. But when we realize that Jesus loves us no matter what we do, we begin to start living for Him. In all that we do, we do it for Him—*not to gain His love, but as a response to it.* Living to please Jesus is simply an act of returning His love. As our love for Jesus increases in our lives, we learn how to do all things as unto God. In this, we find tremendous freedom and excitement. Not only is our heavenly Father surprisingly easy to please, but He is also ever-present to strengthen, guide, and ensure the success of our efforts. The Bible encourages us with the promise, "I can do everything through Him who gives me strength" (Philippians 4:13).

# Against Such Things There is No Law

*C*hloe was not in the bedroom, for she hadn't expected to be needed so early and was down in the kitchen enjoying a chat. Elsie had to ring for her, and while the child waited, she reviewed in her mind the happenings of the day. She always did this before bed, but rarely was her retrospect so painful. Her tender conscience told her that she had more than once indulged in wrongful feelings toward her father. She had allowed Lucy to speak disrespectfully of him, and by her silence, she'd given the remarks her own tacit approval. Worse, she had complained about him herself.

Tearfully, she murmured to herself, "How soon I forgot the lesson Papa taught me this morning and my promise to trust him without knowing his reasons. How can he love me when I'm so rebellious?"

"What's the trouble, darling?" Chloe asked as she came in. She took Elsie on her lap, cradling the child's head as she said, "I can't bear seeing you so upset."

"I've been so bad today, Aunt Chloe. I'm afraid I'll never be as good as Papa wants me to be. I know he's disappointed with me because I disobeyed him today," Elsie said, as her tears rolled down her cheeks.

> "Then you must go to the throne of grace and tell the Lord Jesus about your troubles," Chloe said. "Remember what the Bible tells us: 'If anybody does sin, we have one who speaks to the Father in our defense — Jesus Christ the Righteous One.' Speak to Jesus, darling, and ask Him to help you trust your Papa and obey him even when you don't understand his reasons."
>
> —*Elsie's Endless Wait*, pages 92–93

Every age group has its particular challenges, but in some ways being an adolescent is probably the most difficult. You're no longer children, and yet, you're not adults either. Though this is an exciting time, it's also filled with frustration. The expectations of others, and even your expectations of yourself, seem to change and, far too often, prove well out of reach. If you're like most of us, you're reminded daily of your imperfections.

Another frustration you may face is that no one seems to understand you. Though you may have family and friends around you that love you, it is possible to feel very alone. No matter how much you tell them, there will, at times, be things in your heart that you can't explain in words—things that only Jesus can understand. *This is why it is so important to spend time getting to know the Lord.* He is the One to whom you can tell all your troubles, with whom you can share your innermost secrets, and from whom you can always get advice. He is the perfect Friend, and He will always love you—no matter what!

Though Elsie Dinsmore is a fictitious character, her life's story is a great example of how God's love can see us through the challenges of everyday life. Elsie learned from a very young age that she needed the help of God on a daily basis—in every area of her life.

Elsie wasn't perfect. Although she was very virtuous, she was not flawless or without fault. She didn't have all the answers. She did not possess perfect wisdom or perfect understanding of the Scriptures or the issues of life. And of course, Elsie was not without sinful desires and sinful indulgences. Elsie made mistakes, just like the rest of us.

 **Remember, God looks at our hearts. His focus is not necessarily on all the dos and don'ts of our outward behavior. On the contrary, He's looking for something even more important—a heart of love.**

The Bible tells us in 1 John 4:16 that "God is love." He is looking and longing for people like Elsie who will love Him with all of their heart. Love—your love for God and God's love for you—is what makes the difference in our lives!

As we discussed previously, Jesus summarized all of the hundreds of requirements of God's law in just two requirements. He said, "'Love the Lord your God with all your heart and with all your soul and with all your mind.' This is the first and greatest commandment. And the second is like it: 'Love your neighbor as yourself'" (Matthew 22:37–39). Love fulfills every rule!

For all of us, there are times when we will fail to walk in the fruit of the Spirit. James 3:2 says, "We all stumble in many ways." Sometimes we will make wrong choices and temporarily fail in our spiritual walk. But because of our love for the Lord, though we may feel awful, we will not give up. We will repent before the Lord (and others, if necessary) and try again. *It is this kind of heart—one that truly and deeply desires to love God and walk in His ways—that God loves.*

By now, you are, no doubt, well-acquainted with the nine dimensions of the fruit of the Spirit that will continue to grow in us our whole spiritual life long. As a final reminder of what each of them means, fill out the chart below and write down their reverse or opposite. Let this list serve as a reminder of areas where you need to walk in self-control.

| FRUIT OF THE SPIRIT | ITS OPPOSITE |
| --- | --- |
| love | |
| joy | |
| peace | |
| patience | |
| kindness | |
| goodness | |
| faithfulness | |
| gentleness | |
| self-control | |

The Bible assures us, in Romans 8:9, that we are controlled not by the sinful nature but by the Spirit, if the Spirit of God lives in us.

**Ever before us, we have a choice: we can do things our own way, according to our sinful nature or our "flesh." Or we can "walk in the Spirit," which means doing things God's way *with the help and power of His Holy Spirit*. This is not a one-time choice, like asking Jesus into our hearts. It is an everyday choice for those of us who have already given our hearts to Jesus.**

Now, to summarize what we have learned in this study guide, answer the following questions:

Based on what you have discovered in *Elsie's Life Lessons*, what was the source of Elsie's godly virtues?

If you have accepted Jesus Christ as your Savior, what spirit dwells inside of you?

Even though you need to *choose* every step of the way to be obedient to God, if you focus your heart on loving Him, what power is available to help you?

If you are a Christian and the Holy Spirit is living in you, what is growing inside of you?

How can you promote the growth of the fruit of the Holy Spirit in your life?

In everything that we do, every day of our lives, with every thought and every decision, as we choose to put Jesus first, He provides ample love, joy, peace, patience, kindness, goodness, faithfulness, gentleness, and self-control for us to walk in a manner worthy of our high calling in Christ (Ephesians 4:1).

 **If you find that any fruit is lacking in your life, return to your love relationship with the Lord.**

It all begins with love—your love for God and His love for you. Love is the birthplace of all that is His. When you return to that intimate place in your relationship with Jesus, the light of His love will pour into your heart and shine through your life to touch the lives of others with the fruit that comes from God.

Look back over this chapter. Ask the Holy Spirit to show you the most important things He wants you to remember. Put a star beside those truths and, in your own words, summarize below what He showed you.

Rewrite your thoughts as a prayer, asking God to help you grow and apply the truths He's taught you throughout the chapter.

Write out the memory verse for this chapter:

Write out Galatians 5:22–23, the memory verse for our entire study guide:

# Check out
# www.alifeoffaith.com

- Get news about Elsie

- Join The Elsie Club

- Find out more about the 19th Century world Elsie lives in

- Learn to live a life of faith like Elsie

- Learn how Elsie overcomes the difficulties we all face in life

- Find out about Elsie products

# A Life of Faith: Elsie Dinsmore

*"It's Like Having a Best Friend From Another Time"*

# Collect our other
# *A Life of Faith*™ Products!

## *A Life of Faith: Elsie Dinsmore*

Elsie's Christmas Party:
How to Plan, Prepare and Host an Old-Fashioned Christmas Party
ISBN: 1-928749-52-6

Elsie's Daily Diary (A Personal Journal for Girls)
ISBN: 1-928749-50-X

Dear Elsie — Answers to Questions Girls Ask
ISBN: 1-928749-55-0

### with many more to come!

For information about Elsie Dinsmore and her faith, visit our Web Site at:

### www.alifeoffaith.com

Mission City Press, Inc., P.O. Box 681913, Franklin, TN 37068-1913

# Elsie's Life Lessons Scripture Memory Cards

It is very important to think and memorize the Lord's thoughts—the Word of God. This was one of the greatest "secrets" behind Elsie's amazing Christian walk. By doing so, you will know the Lord better and become more like Him. As Romans 12:2 promises, you will be *transformed* by the renewing of your mind!"

But the fruit of the Spirit is love, joy, peace, patience, kindness, goodness, faithfulness, gentleness and self-control.
—GALATIANS 5:22–23

Be kind and compassionate to one another, forgiving each other, just as in Christ God forgave you.
—EPHESIANS 4:32

Love is patient, love is kind. It does not envy, it does not boast, it is not proud. It is not rude, it is not self-seeking, it is not easily angered, it keeps no record of wrongs. Love does not delight in evil but rejoices with the truth. It always protects, always trusts, always hopes, always perseveres. Love never fails.
—1 CORINTHIANS 13:4–8

Dear friends, I urge you, as aliens and strangers in the world, to abstain from sinful desires, which war against your soul. Live such good lives among the pagans that, though they accuse you of doing wrong, they may see your good deeds and glorify God on the day he visits us.
—1 PETER 2:11–12

Consider it pure joy, my brothers, whenever you face trials of many kinds, because you know that the testing of your faith develops perseverance. Perseverance must finish its work so that you may be mature and complete, not lacking anything.
—JAMES 1:2–4

Let love and faithfulness never leave you; bind them around your neck, write them on the tablet of your heart. Then you will win favor and a good name in the sight of God and man.
—PROVERBS 3:3–4

Do not be anxious about anything, but in everything, by prayer and petition, with thanksgiving, present your requests to God. And the peace of God, which transcends all understanding, will guard your hearts and your minds in Christ Jesus.
—PHILIPPIANS 4:6–7

Your beauty should not come from outward adornment, such as braided hair and the wearing of gold jewelry and fine clothes. Instead, it should be that of your inner self, the unfading beauty of a gentle and quiet spirit, which is of great worth in God's sight.
—1 PETER 3:3–4

As a prisoner for the Lord, then, I urge you to live a life worthy of the calling you have received. Be completely humble and gentle; be patient, bearing with one another in love.
—EPHESIANS 4:1–2

For God did not give us a spirit of timidity, but a spirit of power, of love and of self-discipline.
—2 TIMOTHY 1:7